Illuminating DARK VALLEY

Pauline Henning

720 496 2173
phennco@gmail.com
Pauline Henning

Copyright © 2023 by Pauline Henning

All rights reserved. No part of this publication may be reproduced, distributed, or transmitted in any form or by any means, including photocopying, recording, or other electronic or mechanical methods, without the prior written permission of the publisher, except in the case of brief quotations embodied in critical reviews and certain other noncommercial uses permitted by copyright law. For permission requests, write to the publisher at publishing@kingdomwinds.com.

First Edition, 2023
ISBN: 978-1-64590-052-8
Published by Kingdom Winds Publishing.
www.kingdomwinds.com
publishing@kingdomwinds.com
Printed in the United States of America.

PRAISE FOR
Illuminating Dark Valley

From the beginning, this book was very hard to put down. Pauline has a real talent for making the Scalini family and the valley come alive with descriptive verbiage and heart. It will appeal to all ages, especially young women adventuring out into their young adult lives. It is unique in its storyline and character development. Kudos to Pauline for her perseverance in bringing this story and family off the pages into authentic, original, dynamic, imaginative writing. You will no doubt wish you had bought two, one to give away! Looking forward to the sequel!!

— Bev Gadbois, Editor, Hersher Pilot

Table of Contents

CHAPTER 1: Who Would Have Thought?   9
CHAPTER 2: Mica Will Do It!   19
CHAPTER 3: Growing Pains   25
CHAPTER 4: More Clues & Miss May   35
CHAPTER 5: Conning the Cousins   43
CHAPTER 6: The Road to Milan   53
CHAPTER 7: The Long Trek Home   67
CHAPTER 8: The Landing of the Entourage   75
CHAPTER 9: Mudslide   83
CHAPTER 10: Python or Not?   89
CHAPTER 11: Unraveling Memories   99
CHAPTER 12: Now What?   111
CHAPTER 13: The Investigation   119
CHAPTER 14: The Stinging Truth   129
CHAPTER 15: And the Verdict is?   145
CHAPTER 16: La Fine   163

ABOUT THE AUTHOR   169

Dedication

This book is dedicated to my six siblings with whom sharing life was often adventurous and sometimes mysterious.

Acknowledgments

IN APPRECIATION FOR THEIR ENCOURAGEMENT AND SUPPORT:

Tim Henning

Kathy Rudy

Beverly Gadbois

Nadine Young

H.S.

CHAPTER 1
Who Would Have Thought?

Who would have thought something so simple would be the solution to something so complex? Had I known my silly teenage insecurity would spark such a momentous invention, I'd have done it sooner!

It started on a sparkly spring day as I followed Pa's footsteps to the field to help tend the sheep. Trying unsuccessfully to walk in his footsteps put me close enough to Pa's back with his familiar tweed wool coat saturated in cigar aroma, which I have grown to love. It was the only coat I'd ever known him to own. Boots crunching through the newly fallen snow gave me the vague sense of marching to war, even though I couldn't imagine that in Dark Valley, especially on days like today when heaven seemed to touch Earth. The sun gave me a sense of wonder as it ricocheted perfectly off the lightly falling flakes, refracting into a million shards of color. The phenomenon so surreal yet tangible bonded Pa and I in a way no one else could enjoy.

I knew the drill. Take Jeb, the Australian Sheepdog, up the hill to herd the sheep back down to feed. Jeb could have handled it himself, but it never worked out that way because Pa had come to rely on me, maybe because we did have this special connection. Ever since Ma passed, I became Pa's confidante. I didn't mind and felt honored that he picked me to consult. Plus, lending a listening ear was the least I could do after all he'd done for us. Raising seven children alone under normal circumstances would be challenge enough. Adding six months of frigid weather in continual darkness made it heroic. Living in this isolated mountain village was all I'd ever known except for occasional visits to Milan, the nearest city. Despite our struggles, I wouldn't want to live anywhere else. I loved our life here in Dark Valley.

Like I was a good listener for my Pa, that's what Jeb was for me. I could be talking to Jeb for an hour, and he'd sit there as if I were the most interesting person in the whole world. He had understanding eyes, one blue and one brown, coupled with his crooked ear, flopped over always in my direction. His serene, attentive demeanor made me think he believed everything I said was brilliant. Pa brought Jeb back from Milan when he was just a pup. Instead of being an outside dog to help with herding and protecting, he ended up inside. He was often found under the dining table, competing for fallen scraps with Choo Choo, the farm cat. Choo Choo was supposed to kill the mice, but she wasn't much of a hunter. She liked to play with the mice and let them go, which totally defeated her life's purpose. But you can't teach a lover to be a fighter in animal or man, so there's no sense trying.

Jeb snuck in front of the fire in the sitting room from under the table, and then Jeb followed me upstairs to sleep under my bed. He seemed to understand the importance of being inconspicuous to remain in the house. However, it was challenging in our small home, especially in the tiny bedroom I shared with three other sisters. Our room was directly at the top of the stairs, with my bed being first, smack dab in front of the entrance, which had no door. It was reasoned that since I had to be up first to feed the sheep, I should be closest to the door to not wake the others. At first, no one noticed Jeb, who usually slipped under my bed. Until one night, Jeb, half asleep, nuzzled Eileen's arm by mistake, thinking it was mine. You would have thought there was a robber in the house the way she screamed, which woke everyone except, of course, the boys. They would have slept even if a freight train were chugging through the living room. Pa, however, came straight away, and once he saw it was only Jeb, I suppose he was relieved it wasn't a robber, so Jeb got to stay.

Jeb was a good listener but not so good at offering counsel or advice. For that, I tried to guess what my Ma would have said. So, when I saw Ma's old compact sitting atop Eileen's dresser, I felt no regret in borrowing it the next morning. Ma always used to say the exact thing I needed to hear. Her precise words satisfied me without feeling lectured. I needed her now more than ever to answer my questions about how to look pretty. Sneaking a hurried peek in the small round mirror confirmed my worst fears about my beastly appearance. I quickly drove the compact into my pocket, knowing I would have uninterrupted time while herding the sheep for closer inspection.

Eileen, waking unusually early, rummaged through the dresser drawers. "Where is that thing? It was right here last night. Where did it go? Lily, Sophie, have you seen my compact?"

"Your compact?" I mumbled under my breath. "Hardly."

"Tia, did you take it?" Eileen screeched. Halfway down the steps with Jeb bouncing at my heels, I pretended not to hear her. We both made a clean exit. I sighed happily, escaping before needing to reply.

Just coming out of the dark season, I was relieved, as usual, to have made it. As the days' light lengthened, our spirits lifted. Half a year of veritable darkness left us starving for sunlight. We longed for it like an overdue, pregnant mother-to-be yearned for delivery. The sun slowly creeping over the top of the mountains gradually increased daylight, starting with two or three hours of sunlight to a full sixteen hours by the middle of June.

"You want some breakfast?" Pa asked as he handed me a bacon and egg sandwich.

"Thanks, Pa." I held the steaming sandwich in my hand. Not having the heart to reject his gift, I accepted it reluctantly.

"You better eat it before it gets cold," Pa reminded me, seeing I hadn't taken a bite yet.

"Yes, Pa," Yoke oozed down my chin with the first bite. I was glad now as the warmth edged into my empty belly. Sometimes, Pa knew what I needed before I did.

Our trek to the sheep was easier today as the deep snow drifts had begun to melt. Up on the hill with Jeb, I pulled out the compact to see if the makeup would cover these hideous freckles. "Oh, mio Dio," if I could only tame this twisted mess of hair, I would be the happiest girl in the world. It never occurred to me to do anything except weave the thick, red, coarse thatch into pigtails. To ask for help seemed futile since my other three sisters had smooth, straight hair. "What happened to me?" I often wondered about that and other ways in which I seemed so different from the rest of my siblings.

Pa yelled up to me from below, "What was that?"

"What do you mean?"

"That. There it is again. Like a reflection of the sun hitting me in the face. How are you doing that?" Pa asked in a loud voice.

"I'm not doing anything. What are you talking about?"

I was unsure of what he was seeing and uncertain of what I had done to cause him to ask me how I had done it.

Finally, it dawned on me what had happened. The mirror had reflected the sun down to Pa. Scrambling to my feet to help Jeb with the sheep, I plunged the compact back into my pocket and got on with the task at hand. I didn't want Pa to know I had the compact in case it got back to Eileen.

Sean, the sheep, had snagged his head in the briers again. I'm not sure why he was so susceptible to that since, usually, sheep have very good memories. You'd think he'd remember where the briers were located and not to do something so stupid and mindless again. But I think some lambs get to grazing and lose track of their surroundings. Once, Sean got his head entangled to such an extent that he couldn't get it out. He must have been in that state most of the night because he seemed half-dead by the time we got there. It was a good thing I brought the clippers that morning to free Sean from prison.

We named all the sheep. There are little things about each one to distinguish one from another. Marabel has a birthmark in the shape of a bell on her ear. Sean reminds me of my cousin Sean, who visits every now and again. They both like to wander off. Clover loves to eat clover and on and on. It's not hard to see the differences when you spend so much time with them.

"Pa, we're missing one," I said.

"How can you be sure?"

"I counted them twice, and we're missing one. I think it might be Mable," I replied, somewhat exasperated.

"We better start looking. Hopefully, a wolf didn't get her," Pa replied.

"Hopefully, she's not having a baby or, worse, having trouble with the birth," I mumbled loud enough for Pa to hear as he came nearer. I knew from previous years that spring is the birthing season.

"Now, don't go thinking the worst. I'm sure we'll find her soon," Pa spoke softly, trying to console me.

But I wasn't consoled. "Mable! Where are you?" I yelled at the top of my lungs. "Mable! Mable!"

Jeb was close by, also sniffing under shrubs and low-hanging branches. With each passing minute, my heart rate increased. Mable had sheepskin like marble, just like her personality—sweet mixed with stubborn. Just as it occurred to me that her stubbornness may be an asset, I heard bleating in the distance and then Jeb barking.

"Jeb, where are you?" I yelled as I ran in the direction of his bark. I knew Jeb's yapping meant trouble since he would never make a sound unless it were an emergency. Behind a grove of bushes lay Mable panting heavily. Pa came up behind me, quickly kneeling and feeling Mable's belly.

"She's in labor, but something doesn't seem right," Pa said, tearing off his coat and rolling up his sleeves. He put his hand inside of Mable, feeling for the lamb.

"Lamb is backward. I'll try pulling its back legs rather than taking the time to turn it around," Pa said.

It wasn't but a few minutes before the lamb's legs appeared. Pa continued pulling on those back legs until the whole lamb came out. He held the baby's head down to drain, wiping the birthing fluid away from the nose and mouth so it could start breathing on its own. Steam rose from the lamb covered in fluid and blood. He pulled out his pocketknife and cut the umbilical cord. The lamb wriggled and sputtered for a minute before attempting to stand up. He must have inherited some of his mother's stubbornness because, after several attempts, he was on all fours hobbling around.

"Way to go, Pa; you did it!" I exclaimed.

"We're not out of the woods yet," Pa responded. "I think the lamb is alright, but I'm not too sure about Mable."

A million questions went through my head. What would we do if Mable didn't make it? How would we get her baby to feed? Was there another ewe in the flock who was currently lactating? Would the new lamb bond with the surrogate mother?

"Tia, run to the house and bring back blankets, an empty bucket, warm water, rope, and your brother, Luca. Make sure it's Luca, and have him bring the gun," Pa said. "We only have a short window to get the lamb to bond with another ewe. I don't think Mable is going to make it."

"I wish I could run faster," I thought as I pulled up the ends of my long dress and tucked it inside my winter bloomers. This freed my arms and legs. I must have looked funny, but I didn't really care if anyone saw me.

Finally, reaching the barn, I yelled, "Luca, Pa needs you to come with me to the north field!"

"What for?" Luca hoisted another forkful of hay in the horse trough.

Out of breath, I sputtered, "Mable had a baby! Something is wrong! Bring your gun!"

"Why do I need my gun?"

"I don't know. Pa just said to make sure you bring it."

Upon returning, I could see Mable still hadn't moved, and her baby was bleating and wandering around.

"Luca, I need you to stay and help me get Mable covered and see if we can't get her milked even though she's lying down. We may need the milk for the lamb. Tia, I need you to go inspect all of the ewes and find one with the youngest lamb. Preferably one who gave birth today or yesterday. Take the baby with you, but don't wipe her off." Pa said.

"The baby's name is Sam, Pa," I said.

"Make sure you leave the baby, I mean Sam, with the ewe you've picked. If we can trick the new mom into thinking this little one is hers, then maybe they will bond, and she will let Sam nurse."

Pa continued turning to Luca, "Luca, cover Mable with the blanket. Then help me get the placenta out of her and into this empty bucket. Then we're going to try to milk her lying down."

I picked up Sam and felt the slimy, sticky amniotic fluid starting to dry on his coat. That and his smell compelled me to hold him away from my chest. Looking for the right mother was sort of like looking for the right spot to dig a well. There were certain things to look for, but ultimately, it was more a matter of intuition. Searching for the smallest lamb in the batch came down to two ewes: Hannah or Chloe. "Please, God, help me to pick the right one," I prayed. "Hannah or Chloe?" Hannah was kinder and more agreeable than Chloe, who was a good mother but, at times, could be persnickety. Hannah was the better choice, I surmised.

Hearing a shot coming from Mable's direction, I assumed Sam was now an orphan. I held back my tears for Mable as I tried to save Sam. I placed Sam down next to Hannah and her newborn. I immediately named her Gladys, hoping she would gladly accept Sam as her brother. It wasn't long until I saw Pa and Luca walking towards me carrying a bucket.

"Did you find the right one, Tia?" Luca asked.

"I hope so. This one here," I said as I pointed to Hannah.

Pa said, "Luca, take the bucket with the afterbirth and hold it up to Hannah's nose. Let her smell it, then pour some of the fluid on Sam and the rest on Hannah's back. Now Tia, put Sam under Hannah's nose so she can smell the fluid on him and guide Sam to smell Hannah's back so he can smell it on her. This may trick each to think they belong to each other because of the same smell."

We watched as Sam smelled Hannah. His constant bleating told me he was starving and a little scared. Hannah bleated back to Sam and didn't budge. She wasn't rejecting him; she was welcoming him to feed. Amazing! Sam found her teat and began to suck. We stood there for the longest time watching Sam nurse, dreading what was to come next.

CHAPTER 2
Mica Will Do It!

Mica will do it! This became one of our favorite chants when something needed to be done that was unsavory. The grosser it was, the more he seemed to like it. Cleaning the outhouse, slopping the pigs, and gutting an ewe were all things Mica liked to do. We tied a rope to Mable's legs and dragged her home.

"Mica!" Pa called when we arrived home.

"Yes, Pa?"

"Get your working gloves, bib, boots, and good sharp knives for gutting Mable, and meet me in the barn in ten minutes."

"Lily, Eileen, Sophie, and Tommy, come out and help package up the meat once Mica has it cut. You'll need all the usual supplies: oiled cloth, heavy string, and sharp knives. You know; we've done this a million times. Whatever chores you were planning on doing today will have to wait until tomorrow," Pa said.

"Yes, Pa."

Mica cut off Mable's head and legs first. Then through her shoulders, he put huge hooks attached to a bar and pulled her into the air. Before beginning the skinning process, Mica let all the blood drain into a bucket below. He then sliced along the legs, then the underside, and lastly, right down the middle. Putting his arms in between the skin and hide, he pulled straight down to sever the two. This came out as one large piece of sheepskin. After drying, it would make a wonderful rug, blanket, or coat for us or to sell at the market in Milan. When all the hide was removed, he sliced Mable down the middle of her underside.

With a huge bucket underneath, Mica ripped her organs out. This was the part I couldn't watch. The stench, along with the sound of tearing and the grotesque mass of organs, made me nauseous. I could never be a nurse or doctor, whereas Mica could with ease. Then he took the remaining carcass down onto a table and sliced it into big pieces. We followed behind, cutting the meat into smaller pieces for cooking.

Once wrapped in the oiled cloth and tied tightly, we put it in a special meat container and placed it in our cold room. The container kept the meat protected from wild animals. Our cold room was dug underground, just like so many people in Dark Valley had. It held the coolness even in summer and didn't let things freeze in the winter. We used this instead of the ice boxes commonly used in the city. When we had more time in a couple of days, we would extend the meat's shelf life by drying one half and salting the rest.

Dinner was full of chatter from the day's events. Feeling sad for the loss of Mable but happy for the success with Sam, I was a mixed bag of emotions. We ate leftovers from yesterday since Eileen and Lily were too busy cutting up Mable, leaving no time to fix a full meal. Luckily, there was plenty of warmed day-old bread and heated lamb stew to fill our bellies.

"Tia, what was that thing you had up on the hill today? It seemed to reflect the sun," Pa asked.

"Ma's compact."

"You had Ma's compact? Tia, that's mine! Give it back!" Eileen screeched. "Pa, make her give it back to me!"

"You ladies need to share your mother's things. They belong to all of us now. She wouldn't want us fighting over them. We can pick another one up from Milan next time we go. How does that sound?" Pa negotiated.

"I get the new one," Eileen volunteered.

"Fine by me," I said, half under my breath.

Tommy looked up from his lamb stew and said, "If that small compact could reflect the sun enough for you to notice, I wonder what a big mirror could do?"

"Tommy, what did you just say?" Pa exclaimed.

"Well, Pa, just think about it. If a little mirror could reflect the sun a little, a big mirror would reflect the sun a lot," Tommy said.

Tommy was our very own handyman. If something broke, he'd figure out a way to make it right. He just seemed to have a "knowing" about things that didn't make sense to me.

"That seems reasonable," Pa replied. "I wonder if we could harness the sun during our dark season to bring light to our little valley. What do you think, Tommy? Would that be possible?"

"I think so. Not sure. I guess I'll have to think about that one for a while," Tommy said.

"You do that, son," Pa smiled, peering over his glasses.

"Pa, tell us again, why did Grandpa come to this place? I mean, I get why he might journey here by accident, but why did he stay? What made him do such a thing? I still don't get it," Sophie, the youngest, asked.

Pa took his seat next to the fireplace and told the story we'd heard many times before. Each rendition gave us a better glimpse of the truth as Pa would remember a key detail previously left out, giving another piece of the puzzle.

"It all started when your grandpa left Milan and started walking. He just kept walking and walking, further and further up the mountain. Took him weeks, maybe months. Story goes he lost track of time."

"We know, Pa, but why? Why did he leave Milan? What caused him to leave? Didn't he have a home there and a family? Why would his family let him go?" I asked.

"I don't think his family knew he left until it was too late."

"Come on, Pa. The story doesn't make sense. Something must have happened. Don't you know anything? Anything at all?" I pressed.

"No, I really don't know anything more than what I've already told you. He left Milan. There was something about his running for mayor of Milan and the other candidate," Pa added.

"Wait, what? Grandpa was running for Mayor of Milan, and then he ended up leaving Milan for good? Well, that's some new information. There's got to be more to the story!" I said, a bit exasperated.

"I guess I never thought that through. You're probably right, Tia."

"Didn't you ever wonder why you were living in an area where it was dark six months of the year, Pa?"

"No, why question what you can't change," Pa said.

"Nothing changes without first questioning, Pa."

"When did you get so smart?" Pa scratched his balding head.

"Goodnight, Pa," I said as I kissed him on the cheek. "Come on, Jeb. It's way past our bedtime. Nothing more to hear tonight."

CHAPTER 3
Growing Pains

"Looks can be deceiving," I thought when I saw another family move to Dark Valley.

"Hey Lorenzo, how're things at the Leone's household? Have any new babies or cousins arrived lately?" I asked my best friend and next-door neighbor while waiting for Jeb to relieve himself in the sideyard.

"How'd you guess?" Lorenzo replied as he flicked the hay from his hair, coming out of his barn.

"'Because you're sleeping in the barn again," I replied.

"Yeah, our cousins from Genoa are visiting for a while. Or maybe they're checking Dark Valley to see if they want to move here," Lorenzo replied.

"They should come when it's dark so they can experience what it's *really* like before they decide to move here," I said.

"No one ever comes when it's dark. They come in the spring or summer, fall in love with the place, and relocate without realizing the difficulty of living in darkness for six months," Lorenzo replied.

Dark Valley only describes half of the year in the valley. In the middle of the year, the valley is transformed into an exquisite display of grandeur with snowcapped mountains and wildflowers swaying in the warm breeze with crisp, clear blue skies as a backdrop. A continual serenade of birds and bees fluttering about gives an ethereal feel to the atmosphere. Coupled with babbling brooks and prancing fawns, one might think they had walked into a fairytale. It is a most magnificent place from April through September. I sometimes wish the valley were named for this part of the year, like Happy Valley, Peaceful Valley, or Sun Valley.

"I know you're right. Some of the families are leaving because they can't handle it. Takes a special kind of person to stay. We need new families; otherwise, we'll end up as a ghost town. Or maybe it'll just be you and me," I chided. "You want to come and see the new lamb born yesterday?"

"Yeah, give me a minute," Lorenzo said.

I didn't mind waiting even though my toes were already tingling from the cold like my heart started doing when I got close to Lorenzo. We'd known each other for as long as I could remember, yet I found myself thinking more fondly of him these days.

"Finally, come on!" I said, fidgeting.

"I barely got out of there. Had to promise to do my chores when I got back," Lorenzo said with his mouth full of breakfast.

I loved how he pushed his thick black hair away from his brow. His smell of hay and fresh air somehow made me feel happy. His awkward, lanky figure amused me in the cutest sort of way. *"Oh my gosh, what is happening to me?"* I wondered. I told myself to calm down. It's only Lorenzo. We talked and laughed as we lazily walked up to the lamb herd. We'd done this many times together, and it never got old.

"It's town hall meeting night. Are you coming?" I asked.

"I don't know, maybe. I'll probably have to entertain the cousins."

"Bring them along. Maybe we'll scare them enough that they won't move here before they go to all that trouble," I said.

"Geez, Tia, I thought you wanted people to move here. Or is it just my family you don't like?" Lorenzo said, sounding miffed.

"No, I didn't mean it like that. I was just thinking about how the meetings can get a little out of hand at times. That's all." I kicked myself in the proverbial behind for saying something so stupid.

"No, but that is a good idea. I'll do anything not to have to play another game of gin rummy," Lorenzo said.

"*Phew. No lasting damage from my unthoughtful words,*" I thought. "OK, sounds good."

"You go ahead," I said as I unlatched the wire holding the end of the fence to the post, pulling it open enough for us to walk through as the sheep walked over to greet us.

"Aw, he's so little. What did you name him?" Lorenzo asked, petting the lamb.

"Sam. Poor little guy almost didn't make it, and this ewe isn't really his mother." I went on to explain the whole event to Lorenzo.

"That's amazing. I never knew ewes would adopt another's lamb. That's cool. Come on. Let's go back. I'm freezing."

"I have a few more things I need to take care of. I'll just walk back by myself and see you at the meeting tonight."

"OK, see you there," Lorenzo said as he turned to leave with his hands in his pockets, almost running.

Most town hall nights were filled with at least one person from each family in the Valley. Depending on the agenda, at least one disgruntled person was usually present. Despite the cold outside, I wondered if tonight would be one of those "heated" evenings. I finished breaking up the ice in the water troughs and adding feed to the other troughs. I made a mental note to bring up more hay tomorrow for the three-sided shed where the lambs gathered during the freezing nights as I hurried home to prepare for the evening.

"Eileen, did you remember the refreshments? Tia, do you have my satchel for the meeting?" Pa asked. "My glasses, where are my glasses?"

"They're on your head, Pa," I said. He reached his hand up to his head.

"Oh, there they are. Let's go," said Pa. "You look nice, honey. What are you all gussied up for, or should I say who?" I was blushing and glad Eileen was busy getting the drinks so she wouldn't tease me.

Town hall nights gave us all a chance to get dressed nicely. Not as nice as, say, Sunday church, but nicer than weekly work clothes. I wore my bonnet and laced boots, a nice cardigan, and a floral gingham skirt. I wondered if Lorenzo would notice.

Many people were already there as we walked in. Nothing would start without Pa since he was the mayor. He'd taken over once Grandpa was too old. A picture of Grandpa hung on the wall with an inscription underneath: Rubus Scalini, founder of Dark Valley. Being a descendant was usually a blessing, but sometimes it felt like a burden since more was expected of us in character and duties. I always sat next to Pa and took notes during the meeting.

"It's town hall meeting night. Are you coming?" I asked.

"I don't know, maybe. I'll probably have to entertain the cousins."

"Bring them along. Maybe we'll scare them enough that they won't move here before they go to all that trouble," I said.

"Geez, Tia, I thought you wanted people to move here. Or is it just my family you don't like?" Lorenzo said, sounding miffed.

"No, I didn't mean it like that. I was just thinking about how the meetings can get a little out of hand at times. That's all." I kicked myself in the proverbial behind for saying something so stupid.

"No, but that is a good idea. I'll do anything not to have to play another game of gin rummy," Lorenzo said.

"Phew. No lasting damage from my unthoughtful words," I thought. "OK, sounds good."

"You go ahead," I said as I unlatched the wire holding the end of the fence to the post, pulling it open enough for us to walk through as the sheep walked over to greet us.

"Aw, he's so little. What did you name him?" Lorenzo asked, petting the lamb.

"Sam. Poor little guy almost didn't make it, and this ewe isn't really his mother." I went on to explain the whole event to Lorenzo.

"That's amazing. I never knew ewes would adopt another's lamb. That's cool. Come on. Let's go back. I'm freezing."

"I have a few more things I need to take care of. I'll just walk back by myself and see you at the meeting tonight."

"OK, see you there," Lorenzo said as he turned to leave with his hands in his pockets, almost running.

Most town hall nights were filled with at least one person from each family in the Valley. Depending on the agenda, at least one disgruntled person was usually present. Despite the cold outside, I wondered if tonight would be one of those "heated" evenings. I finished breaking up the ice in the water troughs and adding feed to the other troughs. I made a mental note to bring up more hay tomorrow for the three-sided shed where the lambs gathered during the freezing nights as I hurried home to prepare for the evening.

"Eileen, did you remember the refreshments? Tia, do you have my satchel for the meeting?" Pa asked. "My glasses, where are my glasses?"

"They're on your head, Pa," I said. He reached his hand up to his head.

"Oh, there they are. Let's go," said Pa. "You look nice, honey. What are you all gussied up for, or should I say who?" I was blushing and glad Eileen was busy getting the drinks so she wouldn't tease me.

Town hall nights gave us all a chance to get dressed nicely. Not as nice as, say, Sunday church, but nicer than weekly work clothes. I wore my bonnet and laced boots, a nice cardigan, and a floral gingham skirt. I wondered if Lorenzo would notice.

Many people were already there as we walked in. Nothing would start without Pa since he was the mayor. He'd taken over once Grandpa was too old. A picture of Grandpa hung on the wall with an inscription underneath: Rubus Scalini, founder of Dark Valley. Being a descendant was usually a blessing, but sometimes it felt like a burden since more was expected of us in character and duties. I always sat next to Pa and took notes during the meeting.

I carried any papers or documents we might need, such as the town's by-laws. On the other side of Pa sat Lorenzo's dad, Ed Leone, the sheriff, and Gus Greco, the town manager. We all sat at a long table at the front of the large room in front of the stage facing the audience.

Mr. Greco called the meeting to order. "All rise," he bellowed.

Mica and Luca walked down the center aisle. Mica carried the Italian flag with one large green stripe, a same-sized white stripe, and a red stripe at the end. Luca carried the blue town flag, with the name Dark Valley across the top, mountains outlining the backdrop, pictures of a lily, an Italian Sparrow, and a strawberry tree branch—all symbols of Italy. They stopped in front of us and stood still, facing the audience as we all said the national anthem:

> Brothers of Italy, Italy has awakened; Scipio's helmet she has put on her head. Where is the Victory? Offer her the hair; because slave of Rome, God created her.
>
> Let us unite! We are ready to die; Italy called.
>
> We have been for centuries stamped on, and laughed at, because we are not one people, because we are divided. Let's unite under one flag, one dream; To melt together; Already the time has come.

Before Mr. Greco could call up the first item on the agenda, Mr. Waller stood up, yelling, "What are you going to do about the road washout near my house? Why hasn't the road task force been out to fix it?"

"Roads are fourth on the agenda tonight, Mr. Waller. We will get to that then," Pa spoke with authority.

"I vote we put it first on the agenda! Is there a second?" Mr. Waller shouted.

"Second." Mr. Waller's next-door neighbor, Mrs. Corner, raised her hand in agreement.

"Mr. Gallini's bull got loose from his yard and nearly killed my Lucy trying to mate with her. This is the 3rd time it's happened. I propose I be first on the agenda due to the number of times this has happened, and nothing ever gets done about it!" posed Mr. Logno.

"Now, now, people. We'll just stick to the agenda the way it's stated. We can't go rearranging things at the simplest whim," Pa insisted.

I saw Lorenzo and his cousins slip onto the balcony as I peered up for a split second from my note-taking. I could hear Eileen and the other ladies chattering in the kitchen off to the side of the auditorium, preparing the refreshments for after the meeting. Being the stenographer, I taught myself to write words in a shortened version. I usually omitted unnecessary letters, like vowels or letters not phonetically heard—just enough letters to know what it meant. I would use abbreviations for people's names, like RS for Rubin Scalini. Later, I rewrote the shortened version in a way that everyone could understand. These records are stored for many years in the basement of the building just in case there was ever a disagreement about what happened during a meeting.

The different committee heads of the town would sometimes join us at the table if they needed to report or present on a matter. There were only two paid positions, Gus's and Ed's, while everyone else volunteered. The town agreed to pay Gus and Ed since their positions were full-time and required being on-call any time, day or night. Every person brought their monthly fees to pay the salaries. Granted, sometimes payments were made with a chicken or a pie, but most people were agreeable to the payment. This allowed everyone to feel free to call on either of them whenever or for whatever town-related reason came up. Gus and Ed were kept plenty busy.

I glanced up from my notes just in time to see Doug Duce and his son take a seat at the back. I elbowed Pa to make sure he saw too. Pa nodded in recognition. We both knew those two were like the rooster in the hen house. It wasn't long before Doug stood up and objected to the proposal to fix the washed-out road. I'm wondering why anyone would oppose this.

"On what grounds are you objecting, Doug?" Pa asked.

"If you just fix the road and not the source of the problem, it's going to happen again. Dougy and I can build a ditch to divert the water away from the road so's it doesn't happen again. Here's my proposal," Doug walked up and handed it to Pa.

"That's a brilliant idea, Doug, but the road crew has already figured that into fixing the road at a fraction of the cost you'd charge. Why would we hire you when the road crew will do it at minimal cost?" Pa inquired.

"Because Dougy and I will do it so much better than your lame road crew. They're horrible at everything they do. If you don't give us the contract, there's no telling what might happen the next time there is torrential rainfall!" Doug bellowed.

I felt my muscles stiffen up my back through my shoulders and take up residence in my neck. The headache I always have the day after a town council meeting felt like it would be a migraine this time.

Pa and Ed stood up. "Doug Duce, haven't you learned anything yet? Bullying never gets you anywhere. We'll continue with the next agenda item," Pa said.

"You'll be sorry!" Doug shouted as he and his son stomped out of the hall.

The crowd seemed to sigh with relief as the two left. Yet I sensed we all wondered if the threats were real. So far, Doug hadn't followed through, but the wiggle at the back of my mind kept me attentive to the possibilities. The rest of the meeting proved less stressful once the Duces left. Mr. Gallini was told he would be fined if his bull ever got out of the fence again. Mr. Logno agreed to keep Lucy on the far side of the field, as far away from the bull as possible.

"Good job tonight, Tia." Lorenzo stood holding a cup of lemonade for me as I put away my things.

"Thanks. How did you know I needed this?" I asked, gulping down the drink. Wiping a drip from my mouth, I tried to also say hello to the cousins. The less-than-graceful introduction left me feeling awkward and silly. But they didn't seem a bit interested, so I sloughed it off and gave my attention to Lorenzo.

"Will you stay for a bit and have some cake, Lorenzo?" I asked, purposefully letting my hand touch his arm. I wondered if he felt tingles like I did at the touch.

"The cousins are itching to get home, so probably not. I'll catch you tomorrow, maybe," Lorenzo squeezed my pinky with his hand, just enough so no one else could see, but that small gesture let me know he felt the same way.

"What did you think about the meeting tonight?" I asked as we walked home.

"I think I'm getting too old for this," Pa said.

"Those Duces are creepy. They tried to get my attention on their way out, but I just ignored them. Pretended like I didn't hear what was going on. I didn't want to give them the satisfaction of my attention," Eileen said.

"Do you take Doug Duce's threats seriously, Pa?" I pressed.

"No, I don't think he'll follow through with them, but you never know. You never can tell what someone will do," Pa said, opening the front door.

Everyone was still awake, waiting to hear the night's news from the meeting. After recounting all the events, Pa asked me about the compact.

"You've still got that compact, right, Tia?" Pa asked.

"Yes, Pa, it's still in my pocket."

"Tommy, I want you to come with us tomorrow morning to check out how that thing reflects the sun. I want your take on it," Pa said.

Luca and Mica chimed in and said they wanted to come, too. Then Lily and Sophie echoed the same.

The next morning on the hill, I repeated yesterday's use of the mirror in hopes everyone could see it reflected below. It was a cloudier day, so we had to wait for the clouds to part. When they did, there was no mistaking the powerful impact of the light on those below.

"Wow, that's amazing, Pa. But what's the big deal? I mean, how is that going to help us? I don't get it," Lily said.

Tommy chimed in, "Multiplying the size of the mirror by 1000 and having it positioned on top of that mountain could mean we'd have daylight for at least a portion of the day. Ultimately, we'll want to figure out a way to get the mirror to move with the sun to give us longer periods of sunlight."

"What are we going to do? Take turns standing up there to move the mirror? And how would we ever get a mirror that big? That sounds more like fantasy," Luca's sarcasm put a dent in what little hope we were feeling.

"Stranger things have happened, Luca. Have you seen pictures of those crazy machines called cars? Who would have ever thought that was possible a couple of years ago?" Tommy said.

Sophie said, "I agree with Pa and Tommy that it's a really good idea. I think anything is possible. Right, Pa?"

"Right, Sweet Pea," Pa replied.

Nobody minded that Sophie was the only one Pa referred to by a nickname. The reason was never spoken, but we figured it was because Sophie was born early. Ma lost her life in giving Sophie hers. She was tiny enough to fit inside Pa's shoe at first. We all held a special place in our hearts for Sophie because she never got to meet Ma. She was the most tender-hearted one of us yet a fierce fighter. And we all treated her as such.

Feeling a ray of hope after testing the mirror seemed to give me a bolt of energy and excitement. The possibilities swirled through my head as I stayed to feed the sheep while everyone else went home.

CHAPTER 4
More Clues & Miss May

Why in the world did Grandpa settle in this place where there are only six months of daylight? This question tormented me periodically. It was explained to me that the valley was situated directly below a range of mountains surrounding it. In the winter, the sun never made it above the peaks of the mountains. Of all the other places to choose from, it seemed this would be the last choice. Talking about it with Pa never gave me much satisfaction.

One day, while rummaging through Ma's old stuff, I came across a journal. I wondered why I'd never seen this before as I carefully opened the leatherbound journal whose pages were faded and torn. At the bottom of the first page was the name Rubus Scalini and the year 1855. I couldn't believe my eyes. This was Grandpa's journal! I burrowed myself in the tiny closet amongst Pa's shoes to get comfy enough to read secretly. The first several pages were Grandpa's rendition of his early years in the valley. He recounted how difficult it was to survive in the environment but also how beautiful, almost mesmerizing, it was. I knew why the entries stopped in October.

Aug. 1, 1855, Spent the day chopping down trees/shaving bark to build a house. Spectacular sunset. Light breeze, sunny, warm. Harvested beans, peas, and cucumbers. Doe and Fawn hung out with me today. Very lonely. I miss Ginta. I wonder if she'd move here with me?

Sept. 1, 1855, Made tar to put in between logs. Nights are cooler. Days are shorter. Competing with squirrels for nuts from the trees to store for the winter. Harvested tomatoes, winter squash, melons, potatoes. Dried peppers, tomatoes, and berries for winter.

Sept. 28, 1855, List for the winter. Only 3 hours of sunlight.

Sheepskin blankets, coat, and boots - ✓
Water - ✓
Food in storage - ✓
Wood for fire - ✓
Grease-soaked wicks for lighting - ✓
journal - ✓
Bible - ✓

"Tia! Dinner's ready!" Lily called up the stairs.

"I'm coming!" I put the journal further underneath Ma's old stuff. I didn't want anyone to find it before I could finish reading it.

Dinner usually consisted of lamb but sometimes chicken, veggies from the garden, and biscuits. Lily made the best biscuits ever. There was always pie for dessert. Tonight was rhubarb pie. Rhubarb was as bitter as winters were cold. Mixing it with gobs of sugar made it palatable, but I often wondered why we even bothered with such a bitter fruit when there were so many sweeter choices.

"How do you think we could make that mirror, Tommy?" Pa asked during dinner.

"I don't know, Pa. Do you have any ideas?" Tommy responded.

"I've been thinking about it all day. I'm wondering if there would be someone in a bigger city with connections to engineers who could help us," Pa said.

"Like whom, Pa?" I chimed in.

"I don't know. Maybe we could do some inquiring the next time we go to Milan for supplies," Pa responded.

"Good idea. Can I go?" I asked.

"Me too?" Luca added.

"Me three?" Tommy added.

"I really need to go, Pa. There are things that I can only get in Milan—things only a girl needs," Lily asserted.

"And only a girl can pick out," Eileen hinted.

Pa sarcastically said, "What do you suggest, leaving Sophie and Tommy home alone to care for everything?"

Tia and Luca always get to go, and Lily and I never get to go," Eileen stressed.

"Ok then. Tia and Luca, you are staying home with Sophie and Tommy. Eileen, Lily, and Mica get to go this time. But I'll have no arguing or complaining. Got it?" Pa said, glaring at Lily and Eileen.

"Yes, Pa!" Eileen and Lily squealed with delight.

"We'll leave the day after tomorrow. Make sure you bring food for three days with enough clothes. I'll need a list from Eileen of food we'll need to bring back. And one from Luca and Mica of supplies we need for the farm. Everyone may give me a list of three items you'd like me to pick up, and I'll do my best to get them," Pa said.

I was crushed that I couldn't go, but then I thought this would just be an exploratory visit to Milan. *"Pa will have me come when he really needs me,"* I reasoned. *"Besides, teaching Sophie how to tend the sheep might be fun."*

Pa pulled me aside while everyone was getting ready for the trip. "Tia, I'll need you the next time we go. I'll probably be just setting up a meeting this time. Does that make sense?"

"Yes, Pa. No problem. I think I'll teach Sophie how to tend the sheep while you're gone. What do you think about that?" I asked, smiling.

"Brilliant! Yes, she is getting old enough. I have a feeling we'll be busy with other things real soon, and she may have to take on some of your other duties," Pa winked.

Going to town was always an adventure for everyone—those going and those staying behind. While fun, it was also a bit scary. The road was fairly safe, although it sometimes narrowed to a single lane with cliffs on one side and a sheer rock wall on the other. The wagon was packed with stuff, allowing enough room for one person to ride in the back and three up front. This made it a feasible three-day journey: one day to get there, one day in town, and one day home.

"So, you get to stay home this time, huh? Lorenzo chided as we watched the four take off down the dirt road. "Your Pa asked my Da to keep an eye on y'all while he was gone, like normal."

"Eileen and Lily wanted to shop for some girly stuff since they rarely get the chance," I confided.

"Maybe now you'll inherit your mom's compact and not have to share," Lorenzo teased.

"Well, whatever. I guess it would be nice to have that for myself. Helps me to feel close to Ma," Tia responded without revealing any more.

"Do you want to come with us to tend the sheep today?" I asked. "I'm teaching Sophie how to do it. Might be mildly entertaining."

"Sure," Lorenzo replied. "But I'll need to check with my Papa. I'll probably have to bring my cousins along if that's all right."

"I suppose. Have they ever herded sheep before?" But Lorenzo was gone, leaving my question lingering in the air.

It was more like a brigade than a herding crew. Too many people confused the sheep. I couldn't teach Sophie because Lorenzo's cousins were so loud they scared the sheep. The sheep were scattering in all different directions, causing Jeb to run zigzag back and forth over the hill as he tried to herd them into a workable area. I was getting really irritated and frustrated with the whole situation.

"I'm sorry, Tia. I didn't think my cousins would be so obnoxious," Lorenzo apologized.

"See if you can talk them into a game of hide and seek over in the shrub area while I get the sheep down, would you?" I responded with exasperation. The ordeal left no time for me to teach Sophie anything. I considered it a minor miracle when we finally got all the sheep down, watered, and fed. It's true that sheep eat grass, but we have to supplement it with grain so they receive a complete protein.

"Sorry, Sophie. We'll try this again tomorrow without Lorenzo's cousins," I said.

"It's ok," Sophie said with disappointment in her voice.

That evening after dinner, when everything was cleaned up and Sophie was tucked soundly in bed and asleep, I snuck over to visit Miss May. She lived in a tiny cabin in the far corner of our land. Miss May was one of the original settlers of Dark Valley. She'd come as a young lady to help Grandpa and Grandma with life on the farm and the children.

"Miss May! It's Tia," I called as I knocked on her front door.

"Come in, come in," Miss May said from her chair by the fireplace, where I usually found her. The rest of her cabin consisted of a kitchen with a wood stove, table, chairs, and a small bed in the corner hidden by a couple of dressing screens.

"I've brought you some pie, Miss May. Do you want a piece now?" I asked.

"No, just put it on the counter, and I'll have some in the morning. Nothing like pie for breakfast," she chuckled in reply. "But you could fix me a cup of tea, dear, if you don't mind, and one for yourself."

"Yes, ma'am. Can we have your peppermint-chamomile tea?"

"Absolutely!"

Usually, our conversations started with present-day happenings, eventually triggering a memory, and then Miss May would begin sharing about the past. Pa traveling to Milan sparked her to reminisce about the time Grandpa went to Milan to see if Ginta would marry him and return to the valley to live with him. Back then, Miss May was a good friend and roommate of Ginta's in Milan.

"I'll never forget when Rubus showed up out of the blue at Ginta's front door. I didn't know what had happened to Rubus because he went missing after his run for mayor went south. We'd thought maybe he'd been shot by the Burtons, his body buried in the woods somewhere. Or maybe a bear had gotten him. I didn't know what to think or believe. There were so many stories swirling around town," Miss May recounted.

"What do you mean his run for mayor went south?" I asked.

Not answering, she went on with her story. "Then, one day, he showed up at Ginta's front door like nothing had ever happened. Ginta was elated. It wasn't long before Rubus proposed to Ginta in the most romantic way. He disappeared again for a few days without saying a word to Ginta. Then, in the dead of night, he serenaded Ginta with a song he'd written. It went something like this, 'Ginta, my love, if you won't be mine, I'll be forever wandering in darkness, unsure of the way. But if you'll have me, your love will light up my life like the flames of this fire.' At which time, he lit a prepared fire in the fire pit. Ginta accepted with tears, and the two were wed shortly after that. I was shocked Ginta so easily agreed to live with Rubus up here, so far away. Then I was equally amazed that I agreed when they asked me to join them a year later."

"Do you have any regrets, Miss May, of living way up here?" I asked. But before she could answer, she was asleep.

I draped the quilt from the other chair over her, put another log on the fire, and walked home with more questions than I came with.

CHAPTER 5
Conning the Cousins

The trip to Milan was successful, with plenty of goodies and treats for everyone. Lily bought enough fabric to sew a new dress for all the girls, including Sophie's doll. It was the prettiest calico fabric with periwinkle flowers. Tommy picked up a sculpting tool for carving out wooden spoons and cooking utensils. Eileen chose a sleek compact and bright red lipstick, which I thought made her look ridiculous. Mica was excited about fancy goggles to protect his eyes when doing sloppy work, while Luca added a new sharp knife to his arsenal. And I happily kept Ma's old compact.

"How did you like herding sheep, Sweet Pea?" Pa asked the next night at dinner.

"I never herded the sheep," Sophie replied.

"How come?" Pa asked, shoving a piece of mutton in his mouth.

"Well, Pa, the first day Lorenzo brought his cousins up. They were so loud that they scared the sheep all over the hill. We had a heck of a time just getting them down. But it was a good lesson for Sophie on what not to do when herding and how to gather them when many have gone astray. Right, Sophie?" I said.

"Yes, I learned so much, although I didn't actually do any of the herding myself," Sophie replied.

"That's OK, Sophie. There's plenty of time for that. I want you to go with Tia every morning so you can learn and eventually take over that job," Pa said.

"Yes, Pa," Sophie replied with a hint of disappointment.

I did a little dance inside, keeping my delight hidden. I wondered what Pa had in mind for me to do next. But I was elated that it wouldn't be herding sheep every morning.

"I was able to schedule a meeting with the town council in Milan in a month. Tia and Tommy, you'll be coming with me next month to the meeting," Pa pronounced.

"Yes, Pa," we three replied.

"And not a word to anyone about what we're doing. Do you understand, everyone? I mean it! I need to hear you each say 'yes.' I want to have a plan before taking it to our town council for approval. I don't need the town gossiping," Pa commanded.

Each child said, "Yes," reassuring Pa that the secret would remain safe.

"Tia, when are those cousins of Lorenzo's leaving? They are a nuisance, constantly causing trouble in one way or another. I think those boys need a job," Pa said. "Mica and Luca, when are you going to fix the fence lines? Maybe those cousins would want to help."

"Why would they want to help us work?" Luca asked.

"Because you're going to make it seem so exciting and fun that they will want to volunteer," Pa responded with a smile.

"Yeah, right. How am I going to act like it's fun when it's not?" Luca inquired.

"Remember the time I convinced you to take over plowing the hay?" Pa asked.

"You mean you tricked me into trying it?" Luca asked in disbelief.

"Do you remember what I did to make it look like fun?"

"You were whistling and sort of dancing around like you were having more fun than going to the fair," Luca said.

"Right, what else happened?" Pa encouraged.

"Hmm, you said something like you were the luckiest person in the world to be able to plow the hay, which sort of made me wonder what I was missing. I asked you if I could try it because you looked like you were having so much fun," Luca replied.

"Exactly! So, see if you can't do the same thing with the cousins, and we will have *prendere due piccioni con una fava*," Pa said.

"Huh? Kill two birds with one stone?" Luca said, scratching his head.

"Just try it. Or you can fix the whole fence line yourselves. Your choice," Pa said with a smile and walked away.

The next day, Mica and Luca gathered all the supplies needed to fix the fences: barbed wire, wire cutters, spool of wire, needle nose pliers for bending the wire, and heavy, long work gloves. Sheep have died getting caught in the broken barbed wire, and wolves sneak in, so the fences must be maintained.

"How awesome would this be if this works?" Mica mused.

"I'm up for anything that gets me out of this job," Luca said. "I'd rather get a tooth pulled than fix fences."

"Getting poked with the barbed wire hurts worse than hammering a finger. I hate it, too," Mica replied.

Luca and Mica started nearest the house hoping the cousins would see them. This gave Sophie and I a bird's eye view as we fed the chickens.

"Hey Luca, could you hand me the pliers, please? This is the best job I have ever had. I love fixing fences, don't you, Luca?" Mica said, laughing.

"You know it, Mica, I always look forward to the fences breaking so we can fix them. It's so much fun," Luca said jovially, whistling a tune afterward.

"Oh hey, Jake! How's it going?" Mica said.

"Good, what are you guys doing? What's so funny?" Jake asked.

"We just love fixing fences more than going to the fair," Luca said.

"No way," Jake said.

"Really!" Luca said.

"What's so fun about it?" Lenny asked.

"Hard to explain. The only way you'll find out is if you try yourself," Luca said.

"Ok, let me try," Bernard said.

"Only one thing. Once I hand you my tools, you have to finish. You can't stop in the middle," Luca added.

"Are you pulling my leg?" Bernard said.

"Ok, suit yourselves, but you'll never know how much fun it is unless you try it." Mica whistled a tune as if this were the most delightful work he'd ever done.

Bernard said, "OK, I'll do it. I want to see what it's like."

"Here you go, Bernard; you're a lucky guy," Mica said as he handed him the pliers and his gloves.

Pretty soon, Jake and Lenny joined in, too. Mica and Luca showed them how to cut a new piece of wire from the spool and wrap it around the fence on both sides while one held the fence pieces taut. Then, one wrapped the top with barbed wire. Mica was thinking ahead when he brought an extra pair of pliers and gloves for the third person.

"OK, guys, have fun. And remember, you have to finish the whole fence," Mica said.

Sophie and I stared at each other in disbelief, holding back giggles. We kept busy with our heads down as if we didn't notice anything unusual. As we headed back to the house, we waited to laugh out loud until we were far enough from anyone hearing us.

"Hey Pa, it worked! The cousins are fixing the fence," Mica said.

"I feel bad for them. Maybe we should have them over for dinner. It's the least we can do for their hard work," I said. "Good idea, Tia. Eileen, can you prepare enough food for possibly three more people? I'm sure they'll agree to come to dinner," Pa replied.

"Better make it four; let's invite Lorenzo, too."

"I'll have to retrieve more meat from the cool cellar," Eileen grumbled. "And cook an extra pie and bread, too. But no problem."

"Thank you, my favorite sister," Mica gave Eileen a peck on the cheek, which she promptly rubbed off with her sleeve.

"Yuck! Get away from me," Eileen scolded.

"Mica and Luca, you may have finagled a day off for yourselves, but one of you better ride up and check on them. Make sure they're doing a good job," Pa said.

"Right." Luca said, "I'll go first."

An extra table was brought in and lined up with the dinner table. They covered it with Lily's handmade tablecloth and finished it off with cut wildflowers in a jar, creating a beautiful setting. It was almost dusk before the cousins returned, looking exhausted and famished.

"How'd it go out there, boys?" Pa asked as the cousins came in looking sheepish.

"Fine," Jake mumbled.

"Great fun," Lenny grumbled.

"Yes, what they said," Bernard seemed humbled.

"Mica, show the boys where the pump is outside so they can wash up for dinner." Each boy received an at-a-boy slap on the back from Pa as they exited.

I hurried upstairs for a quick look at Grandpa's diary while preparations were being finished. I forgot Lorenzo was coming for dinner; otherwise, I would have stopped reading the diary in time to brush my hair, which had gotten tangled by a clothes hanger in my closet hideout.

People were filling their plates from the steamy serving bowls. The clack and clatter of dishes and spoons made me think I could slip in unnoticed.

"What happened to you, Tia?" Mica laughed.

"What?"

"Your hair is crazy looking."

Peering at my reflection in the window, I patted my hair down. I quickly sat in the only chair available, which happened to be right next to Lorenzo. I glanced up at him, rolling my eyes in exasperation. Under the table, he squeezed my pinky like he had at the town meeting, which softened my embarrassment.

"You boys eat up. There are plenty of extras, right, Eileen?" Pa exclaimed.

You'd have thought the cousins hadn't eaten in a year, the way they kept shoveling down the food. I jumped up to fill the mashed potato bowl and the mutton plate. I needed a break because my heart was about to pound out of my chest from being that close to Lorenzo. I could barely eat, and my thoughts were all jumbled. I avoided conversation in case I sounded stupid. I wondered if he was having the same reaction to me. He did seem unusually quiet. It's hard to say with him, though. He is always so calm and self-assured. I really loved that about him. *"Oh my gosh! Did I just use the word love in the same sentence as Lorenzo? I'm too young for such nonsense,"* I thought.

I noticed Lenny perk up after eating his fill, profusely complimenting Eileen on her cooking. Eileen turned beet red when she realized he had noticed her. My goodness, what was happening? Pa invited the crazy cousins to dinner, which turned into a flirting fest. Then I saw Jake in the kitchen talking to Lily. I shook my head in wonder, thinking Pa must be the smartest man in the whole universe. He managed to have the fences fixed in one day, humbled the crazy cousins, and fostered blossoming love. It was days like today that made me feel all was right in the world.

Part of me wanted Lorenzo and the cousins to stay longer, but another part wanted to get back to reading Grandpa's journal. I had finished reading through his first winter. After everyone left and the family went to bed, I stayed up to talk to Pa.

"Pa, I've been reading Grandpa's journal, which I found in the back of your closet. I hope you don't mind. I was looking through Ma's old stuff when I discovered it," Tia said.

"No, I don't mind, dear," Pa said softly.

"It sounded like Grandpa almost didn't make it through that first winter. He wrote that a doe slept right next to him, warming him. Isn't that amazing that a deer would do that? Do you think that's real or made up? How could a deer know to lie down next to Grandpa Rubus? Apparently, she saved his life. He had run out of firewood and was in and out of consciousness. It made me wonder if something hit him on the head or if he ran out of food. Did he ever talk about that with you, Pa?"

"He didn't talk too much about his early years. I did sense it must have been extremely difficult, though. I mean, think about it. All alone, not realizing that he was about to be in the dark for six months. I'm sure he wasn't prepared for the length and severity of the winter. I guess it's possible that a deer would do that, but highly unlikely. Maybe God sent the deer to save Grandpa's life so we could all be living here today," Pa said.

"I think animals know more than we give them credit for. Oh, and thanks, Pa, for today," I said.

"Why? What did I do?" Pa asked.

"I don't know, Pa. It was just a really good day. Wasn't it the funniest thing to see the cousins so tired and hungry?

That was the best trick ever, fooling them into fixing those fences. I bet they had never worked so hard."

"Sometimes people just need a little dose of reality to make them recognize their humanity. That's all," Pa said.

"Goodnight, Pa." I stooped to peck him on the cheek as he dozed off.

CHAPTER 6
The Road to Milan

"Sophie, you learn quickly. Now, don't forget to count all the sheep. Oh, and don't forget to give Hannah her antifungal medicine," I said as I packed the bag we all took turns using. It was made of oil-treated cowhide sewn on both sides and attached to a wooden frame clasp at the top. Finally, the day to travel to Milan had arrived.

"I know, I know. You've told me a thousand times. I'm not stupid. Plus, you're only going to be gone for three days. What could go wrong?" Sophie replied.

"I'm sorry. I'm rambling. I'm really excited about this trip. I know you'll do a great job."

"What's so big about this trip, Tia? You've been to Milan so many times. I would think you'd be sick of it by now," Sophie said.

"It's not about Milan. It's about what's going to happen when we're there. We're supposed to meet with the town council to ask for help with the mirror project. I'm not sure; it just feels like it's a big deal. Don't you think so?" I asked.

"I guess I'm more focused on learning sheep herding than the mirror," Sophie replied. "I'm glad I don't have to go to Milan. I'm happy to stay home. It's so much work just to get there. Then, once we're there, we have to deal with all of the crowds. It's noisy and smelly. The stench from the gutters makes me gag.

"I know you're right. But I find it fascinating. The different people, shops, smells, and food invigorate me. Plus, if we do get the mirror working, we could have light in December for our Christmas holiday. Think how much easier our lives will be!" I exclaimed.

"I guess I don't believe it will happen," Sophie said.

"You're right to think that. Many things must occur before we can even conceive it as a possibility. We need to find the funding, an engineer who can design the mirror, a construction company who can build it, and those who can maintain it. We'll need extra food, water, and housing for the workers while they're here. The road will surely need to be broadened and paved," I listed.

"Wow, Tia, you've really thought this through. I can see why you have to go and not Luca or Mica. You think more like a man than they do," Sophie replied.

"Really?"

"I mean that in the best way possible, Tia," Sophie quickly responded.

"I wish I could dress more like a guy. It seems so much easier to wear pants. These dresses are so bulky and cumbersome," I said as I shoved the items further into the bag, trying to close the clasp. "Ok, little sister, wish us luck," I said as I kissed her cheek goodbye.

The trip down was more difficult than usual, with spring run-off flowing right down the middle of the path, turning it into a creek in some areas. The bottom of my skirt was soaking wet when I climbed onto the seat, causing the bottoms of my legs to become especially chilly. Pa tried to keep the horses in the middle of the road so the wagon would straddle the creek, which caused the horses to buck and sway, making the ride incredibly bumpy. What a happy sight when Milan came into view, even though we knew from experience that it would be hours before reaching the city's edge.

As we approached the Hotel Rosi, I felt invigorated by its sheer size and beauty. My first thought was to run to our room and clean up. Instead, stepping into the lobby, we were immediately met by the town council's administrator, Miss Clarissa Fiora. Her eyes widened when she saw us, making me feel self-conscious. I could tell she was holding back her shock, presumably at the way we looked. She gave us a strained smile. Pa shook her hand with confidence, introducing me as the administrator for the town of Dark Valley and Tommy as its engineer. Never being considered, much less introduced, in that role, I must have blushed, causing Miss Fiora to smile compassionately. Pa and she exchanged pleasantries as I glanced about the place. There were fancy shops with beautiful dresses, cosmetics, salons, and unique items beyond imagination. I must have been drooling because Miss Fiora asked me if I'd like to pick something out from one of the stores. I was aghast at the thought since I knew we would never have the means for even the smallest item.

Miss Fiora said, "As a gift from the town of Milan to our honored guests, we hoped you would allow us the pleasure of outfitting you for your very important meeting with the town council. I would be most honored to assist Tia in a salon appointment and dress fitting while you two may choose from the men's department.

I was taken aback by her kindness and a bit suspicious of her motives. I may be young, but it's been my experience that nobody gives free stuff unless they want something in return. Miss Fiora seemed so sincere, though, I couldn't resist. Plus, I would love being fitted for a dress and having my hair and nails done. I smiled and nodded vigorously while Pa and Tommy headed for the men's department with not a minute's misgiving.

Miss Fiora said, "You remind me of my niece, who has grown and moved to Sicily. We would often have these types of outings. I rarely see her anymore. Shall we look at the dresses while waiting for your appointment?"

"That must be hard for you, Miss Fiora. I'm sure your niece also misses you," I said.

"Feel free to call me Clarissa."

I felt like a little kid in a candy shop. I stared in wonder at all of the colorful materials and the different styles of dresses on the mannequins, finding it difficult to choose the correct outfit for a meeting. I needed something nice, but not too fancy, so I could wear it tomorrow and also at home. Clarissa helped me find the perfect attire. We decided on a skirt and jacket in the most unique black and brown tweed with a hint of gold with a light-yellow blouse to complement. Clarissa added a pair of low-heeled, tie-up boots to complete the professional outfit. The shop lady took my measurements and said she'd have it fitted for me by tomorrow morning in time for the meeting. We then went into the salon.

"Come back here to the sinks so we can get your hair washed," said the hairdresser.

The warm water cascading over my hair and the peppermint and lavender-scented shampoo made my scalp tingle. It had been a long time since someone else had washed my hair, and I was amazed at how it made me feel like royalty. I could have fallen asleep as she massaged my scalp.

"Miss Tia, time to move over to the cutting chair," Sally, the hairdresser, said.

"What? Oh, yes," I said as I drowsily raised my head and pulled myself up.

I was glad Sally didn't ask how I would like my hair cut because I had no idea. After covering me with a flowery gown, she swiveled the chair away from the mirror and began snipping. Long strands of my red curls fell to the ground. *"What have I done?"* I thought, but I didn't utter a sound. It was too late now, so I had no choice but to trust the process.

I looked up momentarily and noticed an impeccably dressed man in his fifties stop, peering through the hallway window directly at me. Or, at least, it seemed that he was looking at me. Maybe he was looking at Sally. Sally sighed when the man continued walking down the hallway.

"Who was that?" I asked.

"That's Mr. Burton, the owner of the hotel. They say he's so rich that he has a gold bathtub. I say he's so arrogant that he has a heart of steel."

"Oh, my! He looked like he was staring right at me, or should I say through me," I said.

"I know what you mean. His very presence can be unnerving."

"Here you go, dear!" Sally exclaimed as she twirled my chair to face the mirror.

I couldn't believe it was me. I looked about ten years older with the stylish hairdo.

"Well, how do you like it?" Sally asked.

"It's amazing what you've done. You have real talent." I stared at my hair, which now looked like glued waves framing my face, stopping right below my ears. My long locks lying on the floor almost made me cry. My brain said "run" while my heart said "smile." I listened to my heart and plastered a smile on my face, hoping to appear appreciative and grateful that now I looked like every other woman in Milan.

"But do you like it?" Sally asked again.

"It's wonderful," was the best I could say. "Thank you so much. You've done such an amazing job. If I know anyone who wants a good hairstyle, I'll definitely send them your way," I continued as I quickly gathered my things to head for the door.

In the hallway, Miss Fiora was waiting for me. "You look fabulous! Wait till you get your new clothes. Everyone will think you're a socialite from Milan," Clarissa said.

That's what I was afraid of," I thought—but I smiled politely instead. Thank goodness Pa was there to rescue me.

"You look beautiful, Tia," Pa said. "We should probably check into our room to be rested for tomorrow. It's been a big day. And tomorrow will be even bigger."

"I'll be in the lobby at 8 a.m. to help Tia with her outfit. Breakfast is served in the café starting at 7 a.m. It's only a short walk to the town council from here. See you in the morning," Clarissa smiled goodbye.

"What happened to you?" Tommy chided, "You look like a wet..."

"Don't. Even. Say it," I warned Tommy before he could finish his sentence.

Going to the room without eating any dinner, I took a shower and went right to bed. Pulling the covers over my head to block the light, I dozed off for a fitful sleep. I woke early the next day to a shock. Glancing up at the bathroom mirror as I stumbled in, still half asleep, I screamed, "Nooo!"

"What's the matter? What happened?" Pa asked, running in.

"Look at me! I can't go to the meeting looking like this!"

"Oh dear, I see what you mean," Pa replied, inspecting my hair closely.

"Now you look like you have a bunch of tumbleweeds on your head," Tommy said as he entered the now crowded toilet room. "I think I liked the wet cat look better."

"Tommy, you're not helping here. Better to not say anything," Pa said. "Tia, maybe the hairdresser will be in this morning and can have you looking like a model again."

"Pa, I don't want anyone to see me like this."

"OK, ok. I'll walk down and see if Sally or Miss Clarissa is around. Maybe one of them can come up and help. Tommy, you better get dressed," Pa said.

Pa found Miss Clarissa as she was walking into the hotel. "Miss Clarissa, there is a situation we could use your help with," Pa said.

"Mr. Scalini, I wasn't expecting to see you for another hour or so."

"I realize this may be out of the ordinary, but Tia needs some assistance. She doesn't feel like she can come and ask you herself," Pa said.

"What are you asking, Mr. Scalini?

"Her hair that was so beautiful yesterday evening is now like a rat's nest after sleeping on it. She is beside herself with a fret. She won't even leave the room," Pa said.

Miss Clarissa smiled, "I understand. Yes, of course. Let me get a few items from the salon, and I'll be right up."

"Thank you so much. You have no idea how grateful we are," Pa said.

"No problem. Happy to help."

As Miss Clarissa completed the final touches on my hair, I said, "Thank you so much!" as I looked in the mirror. "You've done a fantastic job fixing my hair. I'd better hurry and get dressed, or we'll be late for the meeting. Thank you for bringing up my new clothes from the seamstress, too," I said as I closed the bathroom door for privacy.

"Where's Tia?" Pa said as I emerged from the privy. "Who's this lady in our room?"

Laughing, I said, "Almost didn't recognize you two either in those fine suits. We better get going since these fancy shoes may slow me down."

"Could you hurry up, Tia? Geez, we spent hours waiting for you to get ready, and now you're going to make us late for the meeting because of those stupid shoes," Tommy complained.

"I'm coming as fast as I can," I said, almost tripping on a crack in the sidewalk.

Walking up the long steps to the town hall gave me time to feel the gravity of what we were about to do. My stomach was in knots, and my head was pounding. The doors were huge with long gold handles. Pa held the door for me as we passed into a magnificent foyer. The tiled floors and high ceilings echoed the sounds of voices and footsteps. I was mesmerized by the heavenly picture painted on the ceiling fifty feet above my head. Having never witnessed such beauty, I paused in amazement.

"Tia, come on," Pa insisted, already halfway up the next flight of steps. Snapping out of my daze, I quickly joined Pa and Tommy to enter the meeting room together.

The town council room had high ceilings painted with bright colors of stark figures depicting an active courtroom. The council members were seated in a row of high-backed wooden seats in the front of the room. A cabinet surrounded their chairs at a higher level than the rest of the audience, which promoted the illusion of grandeur. We saw Miss Clarissa wave us to a row, so we slid into the one she'd indicated.

"You are third on the docket," Miss Clarissa informed. "When it's your turn, they'll call your name. Then, you three will go up to the table in front of the room. They have their own stenographer who will be typing everything that is said. But Tia, you should keep your own notes, too, just in case," she insisted. "Don't let them intimidate you. Each one of those councilmen comes from humble beginnings. Just be yourself. I know these guys, and most won't like you trying to look all puffed up. Mr. Scalini, speak loud and clear. Be concise about your idea and what you need to accomplish the project. Any questions?" Miss Clarissa asked, concluding her remarks.

"I was thinking of letting Tommy explain the mechanical aspect of the mirror. Would that be all right?" Pa asked.

"Yes, as long as he speaks up and is succinct," Miss Clarissa said. "Ok, here we go."

"The town council will come to order this sixth day of June, 1910. First on the agenda..."

My heart was pounding out of my chest, even though I wouldn't be speaking. I forced myself to focus despite my brain feeling like a rabbit zigzagging from one end of a field to another. Off to my right, out of the corner of my eye, I noticed Mr. Burton from the hotel sitting by himself. I got a sick feeling in my gut when I saw him, but I couldn't explain why. I wondered why he was here.

Finally, the clerk called our name. Once we were settled, she read out loud the brief of our proposal. Mr. Rosen, council president, spoke first.

"Mr. Scalini, what makes you think we would be able to help you? Won't you need an engineer and a construction company more than a town council?"

"Yes, sir, we will need those things, but we will need financial help and support, and I thought you would like to be part of this adventurous endeavor. It would make a good news story once it's working. It would place you on the map for having the foresight to finance and support this technological breakthrough. Perhaps you could patent and sell the discovery to other mountain towns with similar problems."

"Mr. Scalini, how do you know it's going to work? What evidence do you have to make you think it's a viable solution to your problem?" Mr. Rosen reiterated.

"Well, we've seen it work firsthand when Tia was up on the hill with a small mirror. The sun reflected so strongly from that little mirror, and we realized a big mirror would make an even bigger impact. Tommy, my son, has a very mathematical mind, so he's better at explaining the technical aspects of the proposal."

"We will allow a 2-minute presentation," Mr. Rosen said.

Tommy's voice cracked when he first started, but he soon spoke with such confidence and assurance that it was apparent even the council was impressed. The five members gathered in conference quickly and came back with their decision.

"We regret to inform you that we don't have the finances nor capacity to facilitate your project at this time. Perhaps as our city grows, we'd be able to help at a future date. Or perhaps you could submit your request to a bigger city like Sicily, which has more resources. Again, we're sorry we will not be able to support your efforts at this time," Mr. Rosen said as he hit his gavel, resonating with the finality of their decision.

We were all stunned at the quick, decisive rejection. I'm unsure what I expected, but it certainly wasn't a "no" verdict. We collected ourselves and headed out the back door of the room. Miss Clarissa met us in the hallway.

"I'm so sorry they didn't accept your proposal. I thought you had a good chance," Miss Clarissa said.

"What do we do now?" I asked no one in particular.

Just then, Mr. Burton came toward us. He shook Pa's hand and introduced himself.

"I would like to take you out to dinner tonight. I have a proposal for you that I'm sure you'll be interested in hearing. Say 6 pm in the dining room at my hotel where you are staying?" Mr. Burton asked.

Pa responded, "Tia, Tommy, is that ok with you?"

We nodded in agreement, as if we'd ever say no to such an offer.

"We'll see you then. Thank you," Pa responded.

After Mr. Burton tipped his hat and walked down the hall, Pa turned back towards Miss Fiora and said with a slight smile, "We appreciate your kindness in helping us appear credible."

"Meeting with Mr. Burton may be the connection you are seeking. Be careful, though," Miss Clarissa whispered as she hurried back into the council room.

"Did you catch that, Dad? What did she say to be careful of?" I asked.

"I don't know what she means, but I'll certainly be examining things closely based on her warning. Let's go shop for those items we need before going to dinner," Pa said, not offering a choice.

That evening, I so appreciated my new clothes and hairstyle as we walked into the elegant dining room. Glass chandeliers entwined with lit candles hung from the ceiling throughout the room, creating an amber ambiance. The golden tablecloths, sconced lights, and threaded carpet created an opulence I'd never seen. Elaborate, floor-length curtains complemented the décor embellished with yellow marigolds and a dab of red in the center. It reminded me of what one might expect to see in a royal palace, not a restaurant.

Every table was adorned with matching, offwhite china with a ring of tiny marigolds circling the edge of the tablecloth, napkins, and plates. Real crystal glasses and solid silver cutlery surrounding the plate like sentries completed the magnificent display.

Mr. Burton was already seated with a younger man. He stood and pulled my chair out while introducing his son. "I'd like you to meet my son, Jaden," Mr. Burton said.

Jaden was the spitting image of his father. He, too, was impeccably dressed in an expensive suit. His thick, jet-black hair, combed with oil, was so perfect that it almost looked like a wig. His guarded, polite smile caused me to wonder what he was protecting. He shook each of our hands firmly and yet with reserve. I was surprised by the smoothness of his hands. They obviously had never touched a shovel, gutted a lamb, or fixed anything. I wondered what lifestyle afforded such softness.

"I took the liberty of ordering our meals. I hope you don't mind," Mr. Burton spoke, bringing me back from my musings.

Immediately, servers brought out beautifully arranged plates of decadent food. There were thick slabs of meat covered in a steaming sauce and vegetables cut in curious shapes, including impeccable mashed potatoes. The smaller bowls held elegant mushroom morsels—exquisitely sauteed, blanched, doused with alcohol, and drizzled with molasses. My taste buds exploded like the fourth of July. I wanted ten servings of each, but my belly wouldn't allow it.

Once we were fully fattened, and as the formalities and small talk were out of the way, Mr. Burton began, "I was impressed with your proposal today during the council meetings, and I think I may have an idea that could address your needs.

In addition to owning several hotels, I also own a construction company. I have equipment and resources that could be used to put this mirror in place. Also, I have contacts with engineers who could help us put this whole thing together and, most notably, the financial wherewithal to fund the venture.

In exchange, I would ask that I have total control over the project and that you sell my company 3,000 acres on which I will build a ski hill complete with hotels and restaurants. We will have to iron out the details, of course, but how does the general idea sound?"

Pa said, "Well, Mr. Burton, that is quite a generous offer. I will need to think it over and take this proposal before our town council. Of course, many details must be ironed out before we can sign anything."

"Of course, of course, Mr. Scalini. Maybe I can come up to Dark Valley with a surveyor and an engineer in a few weeks to see if the project is feasible. How does that sound?"

"Two weeks? You move fast, Mr. Burton. We do things a lot slower up in the hills. I'll have to run it by our town council committee so that they are aware of what is going on. I haven't spoken to anyone yet, and this may be a bit of a shock to them. However, I think I can pull it off by then," Pa said.

"Ok, great! It's been wonderful meeting with you, and I look forward to our continued venture," Mr. Burton said with charm.

Jaden rose immediately and fell in line with his father, not uttering a word nor revealing a hint of emotion. I didn't know what to make of these two. There was something not quite right about their impeccable, polished demeanors. I filed that in the back of my brain right next to Sally's and Miss Clarissa's warnings about Mr. Burton.

CHAPTER 7
The Long Trek Home

"You ok, Pa?" I asked as we rode home the next day. "Your silence is making me nervous. What did you think of Mr. Burton's proposal?"

"I'm not sure what to think. On the one hand, this may save our town, or it's possible it could kill the town for good. I didn't anticipate paying such a high price for the mirror," Pa said.

"What do you mean by "high price"? Sounded like a big win for us. Think of how fun it will be to have a ski hill and more restaurants than Sally's Cafe. Plus, it will create jobs. I think it's just what Dark Valley needs," Tommy said.

"That's true, Tommy, if everything works according to plan. But it could also totally change our lives to the point of being unrecognizable and a place we may no longer want to live. Think about all of the different people who will be coming into town. We'll become like a resort area."

"I know. Sounds like a hoot! Nothing ever stays the same. That's what you always say, right, Pa?"

"I guess you're right. It'll be interesting to hear what the engineers determine. They may not be able to build a workable mirror, in which case all of this will be moot."

"Moot? What's that?"

"It means none of this will matter because it's not going to happen. Get it?"

"I guess," Tommy said.

"But what did you think of Mr. Burton and his son?" I asked.

"Not sure," Pa said. "It is hard to read them. Why do you ask?"

"Something doesn't sit right with me, but I can't quite put my finger on it."

"I know what you mean," Pa said. Will you set up a meeting with Gus and Ed for this Wednesday evening at our house, Tia? I'll need to get them up to speed. And can I count on you two not to go spilling the beans about the ski hill and all of that until we see if any of this is really going to work? I mean it; mum's the word. You got it?"

"Can I tell Lorenzo, Pa? I'm dying to tell him, plus his dad will know Wednesday anyway."

"Think about it. What if the whole town finds out about building a ski hill, and then it never happens? How will people respond?" Pa asked.

"Well, some people will love the idea and be really disappointed and maybe even a little angry if it doesn't happen. Others will not want the ski hill and be happy when it doesn't happen," Tommy said.

"Right, and every variant in between. So, it will save us a lot of headaches if we keep that part of the bargain under wraps until we know it will work. We'll hold a town council meeting later and take a vote. Only a majority vote will move the plan forward."

"What if people don't want it?" Tommy asked.

"Well, then we won't do it, or maybe we can negotiate a different deal. I guess we'll cross that bridge when we get to it. So, we can tell everyone that Mr. Burton is coming with some engineers to survey the land for building the mirror, but not the part about the ski hill and restaurant," Pa said.

The ride home was slow and painful. Returning home was usually more difficult with the climb in elevation and our exhaustion. The extra weight of the supplies didn't help, either. I couldn't wait to get home to tell Lorenzo.

Lorenzo was playing fetch with his dog in his front yard as the wagon bounced up the hill past his house to ours. Our house was the last one on the road. It sat back a bit, hidden behind two huge Norfolk pines.

"Hi, Tia," Lorenzo waved as he ran towards us.

"Thanks," I sighed as he grabbed the bag I was holding.

"Oh, mio Dio, what do you have in this? It's as heavy as my dad's tool bag," Lorenzo said.

"I acquired some extra things while in Milan," I said sheepishly.

"Like what, a new flattening iron? It feels that heavy," Lorenzo said.

"More like a curling iron," Tommy said.

"What?" Lorenzo looked confused.

"Never mind him; just help me get it inside, and I'll tell you all about it when you come with me to check on the sheep tomorrow," I said.

The next day, Lorenzo wasted no time in asking me, "Tia, what was in your bag yesterday?" as he reached for my hand.

"Oh, uh," I giggled a bit. That tickle sensation came over my hand as his skin met mine. His unexpected reach made me lose track of where I was and what I was doing.

"Your bag, Tia, what was in your bag?" Lorenzo persisted.

"Tommy was right about the curling iron," I said as I took off my hat for the first time in front of Lorenzo.

"Wow, you chopped off your hair!" Lorenzo exclaimed. "But what is a curling iron?"

As I started to explain, a soft breeze blew the willow blossoms in a whirlwind all around us, creating a surreal atmosphere. The morning dew prevented us from sitting at first, but as the sun rose higher, we lay in the tall, soft grass. I told Lorenzo everything from meeting Miss Clarissa to getting my hair done, from the town council meeting to dinner with Mr. Burton and his son. Lorenzo watched me intently as if he were etching my every word and movement into his mind. I stroked his hand as I explained my disappointment when the Milan Town Council turned us down. Then, I stood up to demonstrate the huge ceilings and grandeur of the hotel dining room and the town council building. Lorenzo leaned back on his arm, gnawing on a piece of grass, enjoying the show.

"So, can you and your dad make it to the meeting at our house on Wednesday?" I asked as we walked back home.

"Wouldn't miss it for the world. I'm sure my dad will rearrange everything else to come," Lorenzo stated.

"And not a word to anyone else about it," I said, not letting go of his hand.

"I know, I know. You've told me a thousand times. I won't have many people to tell after next weekend. The cousins are leaving. They've decided not to move up here.

But maybe they would change their minds if they knew all the changes coming."

"Another family leaving! I sure hope the mirror is the key to keeping Dark Valley alive. I heard the Bianchi's are leaving at the end of the summer. That will be the third family this year. Why can't the troublemakers like Doug Duce leave rather than good families like the Bianchis?"

"You worry too much, Tia; it'll all work out. You'll see."

I turned toward him as he turned toward me. Our lips met and stayed for a few seconds. The moment's awkwardness made us both look at our feet as we turned away and said our goodbyes. The wind took our words and threw them into the air, making them seem non-existent.

"Oh my gosh, this is serious," I thought. *"Did we just kiss?"* My heart felt as if a herd of horses were stampeding through it.

Wednesday night couldn't come fast enough. Eileen was in her element preparing a special dessert for the evening. The strawberry preserves canned from last year's crop made a perfect filling for strawberry tart, which would be topped with homemade whipped cream from cream that had risen to the top of the cow's milk. As much as Eileen often rubbed me the wrong way, I did appreciate her fantastic cooking. The table was cleared of dinner dishes and graced with one of Lily's fancy tablecloths for company. Just as Eileen was an excellent cook, Lily was equally accomplished at sewing. She used the scraps from different projects to create a patchwork quilt of sorts for the tablecloth. Ginghams, plaids, and tweeds combined with lace trim produced an appealing ensemble. The men couldn't have cared less for all of the niceties, but we knew a woman is known by the house she keeps.

"What's with the special meeting, Rubin? I saw Doug Duce stumbling out of Sally's Cafe. I hope he's not fixing to cause trouble like he usually does when he's been drinking. I'd like to keep an eye on him, but I guess this is more important," Gus said.

"Well, if he's causing trouble somewhere, we'll hear about it soon enough. I think you and Gus will find this more interesting. Have a seat. Would you like some of Eileen's famous strawberry tart? Won first place at the town fair last year," Pa said.

Before they could answer, Eileen was dishing up the tart. I sat next to Pa with my notepad and pencil. Lorenzo sat on the other side of me. I hoped he didn't see my hand shaking as I held the pencil to write. He must have seen my nervousness because he started poking me in the side to make me giggle. I swatted his hand away and was grateful for the moment of levity that broke the awkwardness of seeing him for the first time after our kiss. I really loved him for that.

"As you know, Tommy, Tia, and I went to Milan to see if we could get some help building the mirror," Pa said.

"Wait, what are you talking about? What mirror?" Gus acted surprised.

"Don't you remember? I told you about it when we were coming out of church," Pa said.

"Oh yeah, I vaguely remember that. I thought that was just a passing fancy. What's all the fuss? Six months of no sun isn't such a big deal. Heck, I've been living here for almost fifteen years, and I'm used to it," Gus responded.

"Well, maybe it doesn't bother you, but people are leaving because of it. I hear the youngins saying they're going to the city as soon as they can leave home. We've got to do something, or we won't have much of a town left," Pa replied.

"Ok, well, go on. What came of your trip?" Ed asked.

There were lots of "ums" and "ahs" and shaking of heads as Pa told the whole story.

"Mr. Burton is supposed to come two weeks from today with a surveyor and engineer to survey the area and see if it's all going to work. Would be good if you could be involved with the tour," Pa finished.

"What and when do we tell the townspeople about what's going on? You know they'll be asking a million questions when they see these people poking around," Gus asked.

"I've already thought of that. At next week's town hall meeting, we will inform them of the reason for Mr. Burton's visit. For now, we'll leave out the part about the restaurant and ski hill. We'll talk to them about that after seeing if this is feasible. We can hold a special session and take a vote to see if we have agreement from a majority of the people for the ski hill and such. That will cause a major upset in their lives, and some may not want it," Pa said.

"Yes, but I think most will want it, especially the young ones," Ed stated.

"So, are we agreed?" Pa asked.

"I want to get a good look at Mr. Burton," Gus said. "What do you think of him?"

"I'm not sure other than he's rich and has all the connections we need to get the job done. I figure I don't have to like him. You'll be able to interrogate him as much as you want," Pa reassured as he shook the men's hands goodbye.

CHAPTER 8
The Landing of the Entourage

There was no hiding the arrival of the entourage from Milan. Such a splash of grandeur never before seen in our tiny town brought out half the population to witness for themselves.

The crew paraded a fancy red convertible Fiat, complete with padded leather seats and Mr. Burton at the wheel. He was wrapped in a full-length, lambswool-lined leather coat. Upon his head was a leather bomber hat wrapped with goggles and a white scarf. Despite the long drive in the open air, Jaden and his dad appeared perfectly manicured as if just stepping out of the pages of a magazine. The other two men, not as pristine yet professional enough, drove behind in a brand-new truck carrying equipment. I wanted to laugh at the audacious display of wealth but didn't, knowing our needs.

"How was your trip? I hope the ride wasn't too bumpy. I know the roads need some work," Pa spoke apologetically while reaching to shake Mr. Burton's hand.

"Yes, well, nothing we can't handle, Mr. Scalini," Mr. Burton responded.

I wondered if there was a double meaning behind that response. Does he mean he can handle the bumpy ride, or he'll handle fixing the roads? There seemed to be a double meaning to most things Mr. Burton said.

"I'd like you to meet Mr. Sam Ruggiero, the surveyor, and Mr. Don Ricci, the engineer," Mr. Burton said.

"This is Gus Greco, our town manager, and Sheriff Ed Leone. Also, meet our town council members, Mr. Waller and Mr. Gallini. I'm sure you'll be working many hours with these gentlemen if we can come to an agreement," Pa said.

"Do you really think bringing light to our town in the winter is possible?" Mr. Waller asked no one in particular.

Mr. Ricci spoke up, "It's actually very feasible to harness a portion of the sunlight to help you all. It'd be just like if I take this mirror and reflect the sun just like this." Mr. Ricci pulled out a small mirror from his pocket and reflected the sun right onto Mr. Waller's startled face. "Shall we proceed, gentlemen? We have a lot to accomplish today."

"I hope you don't mind if we tag along," Pa said as the four of us hopped into the police car, the only car in town. "Tia, you brought your notepad, right? Take notes of where they are surveying and everything you hear them say," Pa directed.

The Milan crew measured and surveyed every inch of our small town. They took copious pictures in every location, from the top of the hill to the town center, all the way to the neighborhood on the west side. They stopped at Sally's Cafe for lunch. Everyone turned to see the entourage entering as the bell above the door tingled.

"Excuse me, pardon me," Mr. Ricci spoke as the four squeezed by those sitting in the cozy cafe. They seated themselves at the empty four top table in the middle next to the bar. Sally was cooking on a huge stove to the left of the bar, where her daughter, Lucia, was pouring drinks and distributing food. Sally looked out over the whole room as she ladled food onto tin plates, including large slices of fresh homemade bread with herbed oils. We slipped in almost unnoticed and sat at a table in the corner.

"Two pasta alla carbonara and two pasta margherita for table ten," Lucia yelled their order to Sally.

"Table eight, order ready," Sally yelled back.

Sally put the plates on the counter, and Lucia delivered them, not necessarily remembering which order went where. You could see people exchanging plates until the right dish was where it belonged.

This went on from 10 am—2 pm every day. Since there were only two choices, with each day of the week offering the same choices, everyone knew the menu. It had been this way for as long as anyone remembered. Sally cooked all the food the night before, usually consisting of pasta, polenta, risotto, and gnocchi and then a different sauce, depending on the day of the week. Tiramisu and pudding for dessert were also part of the menu. In the morning, she'd come in and start the ovens to heat the food for the day. The routine would repeat itself week after week.

As I watched Burton, he seemed to be working the crowd. He spoke loud enough for everyone in the cafe to hear.

"Have you seen this trick, Jaden?" Mr. Burton asked as he pulled out a deck of cards. He told Jaden to shuffle the deck, pick one card, and look at it. Then he instructed Jaden to put his card back in the deck anywhere he wanted and hand the deck back to him. Mr. Burton showed Jaden the exact card he had chosen. Everyone gasped in disbelief, and Jaden scratched his head.

"How about you?" Mr. Burton motioned to the man sitting at the next table. Mr. Burton astounded him as well with the sleight-of-hand trick. Soon, all the customers near them were stretching their necks to see the show.

I noticed that Burton and friends were served before others who had been waiting longer, and their plates looked fuller, too. As Burton finished his food, he said loudly, "Miss Sally, that pasta alla carbonara was bellissima!" He touched his fingers to his pursed lips like a kiss from heaven.

"Almost better than my chef in Milan. Why, maybe you would like to come to Milan for a couple of days and learn some special cooking techniques from Chef Alonso, all expenses paid. Lucia is welcome to come, too. You can stay in the hotel, and I'll send my car to pick you up and drop you back off," Mr. Burton said.

Looking dumbfounded, Sally responded, "Yes, I would love that. When would that be? It'd have to be on a Sunday and Monday when the cafe is closed," Sally said.

"No problem. Say two weeks from next Sunday?" Mr. Burton confirmed.

"Yes, sure, that would be wonderful. Thank you very much!" Sally exclaimed.

"Good. Then it's settled. Gentlemen, shall we get back to work before the day is gone, or we'll have to rent one of Sally's rooms for the night," Mr. Burton chuckled as he placed a large tip on the table for all to see.

At the last stop, Mr. Burton said. "We'll be heading back to Milan now before it gets any later. Things are looking really good for the mirror to be installed as well as the ski hill and lodge."

Mr. Ricci spoke up, "Yes, agreed. This is an ideal setting and very doable. You're far enough away for people to feel like they've really had a vacation, but not too far that it's difficult to get to. According to my initial calculations, the mirror can be perfectly situated to allow for about 4 hours of sunlight a day during the worst part of the winter and perhaps even six hours in the fall and early spring. I'll have to do some final calculations, but it looks promising. This area is also perfect for many types of recreation. We may even be able to make a skating rink in front of the lodge. This place is a gold mine."

"Yes, well, we mainly just want to help the people of Dark Valley have more hours in their day. Any benefit to us will pale in comparison to the benefit the good people will enjoy with the placement of the mirror," Mr. Burton said.

"Yes, yes, of course," Mr. Ricci and Mr. Ruggiero both agreed in unison.

Rubin asked, "Well, okay then. Can you come to the next town council meeting in two weeks to speak to the town about your proposal? Mr. Leone, Mr. Greco, and I will have to agree to it first, so perhaps you can come earlier that day to give us a chance to read it. Does that sound agreeable?"

"Yes, that sounds wonderful. You have a beautiful place here. I'm really hopeful we can help save it," Mr. Burton said as he put on his leather hat and goggles.

We watched as they sped off. Dust flew in the air as they left.

Waiting for the next town council meeting was like waiting for Christmas. Everyone was speculating how wonderful it would be to have sunlight and not have to see by the light of candles. Not to mention, we were hoping it would help keep the temperature warmer. The information about building the ski hill and lodge had been leaked. This caused an extra surge of optimism that permeated the atmosphere so tangibly that one could feel it. Finally, the day arrived.

A courier brought the documents the day before the town meeting. Pa, Ed, and Gus read the documents very carefully, but not being lawyers, they found some of the language difficult to understand.

"Section 10 bothers me because it talks about Mr. Burton having total control over the ski hill and lodge. That makes me nervous. I don't know the first thing about skiing or running a ski hill. There are a million things that could go wrong," Pa said.

"Since he's the one paying for and building it, he will want to run it. Besides, we'll still have control as the town council if legislation needs implementing. We can always enact new laws. Right?" Ed said.

"Good point unless he runs for town council one day. Then he'd be close to running the whole town," Gus said.

"Exactly my concern, Gus. But I don't think we have any other option at this point. We need to proceed with hope and pray for the best," Pa said.

I was taking notes, but I left that last part out.

Lorenzo picked me up to help me carry the briefcase to the town meeting. Eileen had a wagon full of goodies for the event. Everyone else was dressed in their best clothes. We left early to get a good seat and were surprised to see many people already there for the same reason.

"I wish you could sit with me up front," I said to Lorenzo.

"No thanks, that's your job." But I can sit in the front row and keep an eye on things if you'd like."

"Quick, grab that last seat in the front at the end. I'd feel better if you were near. Moral support, you know," I said.

"I get it, not a problem. Anything to be closer to you!" Lorenzo smiled affectionately.

"Good evening, gentlemen," Mr. Burton said to Pa and the council. "We need another table for the people I've brought with me. This is Miss Belfi, my stenographer, and Mr. Silco, my lawyer. Also, Mr. Pulli, another engineer, to help field questions with Mr. Ricci."

We scrambled to get another table to put next to ours as we all faced the audience. I looked up at the sea of faces staring back at us. We pushed our table all the way to the front to make room for the extra audience. Some people brought their own kitchen chairs, and others came with pillows for sitting on the floor. This was one of the biggest happenings I could remember.

Mr. Burton's presentation was extravagant with colored drawings depicting the ski area and lodge. The pictures taken of the hill showed a drawn mirror on top reflecting the sun to the town below. People presented logistical questions which showed consideration of the impact of such a venture. But in the end, everyone agreed it to be a beneficial plan. Hope filled the atmosphere when the positive results of the vote were announced.

"How do you like living here?"

Looking up from my notepad, I was startled to see Jaden standing there, asking me a question. "I love it here, but it's really all I've ever known except for my occasional trips to Milan. How do you like it so far?" I responded.

"It will be nice once the ski hill and lodge are in. I think I'll really like skiing, although I haven't tried it yet," Jaden responded.

"Will you be helping your Dad with the project?" I asked.

"Absolutely. I want to learn how to construct different buildings. This is a fantastic opportunity for me. I'll be with my Dad every step of the way. I guess we'll be seeing a lot more of each other moving forward since I'm sure you'll be just as close to your father's side as I will be to mine."

"Yes, I suppose that's true."

"What did he want?" Lorenzo asked, handing me a cup of lemonade after Jaden left.

"Nothing really; he just asked if I liked living here. Just small talk," I responded.

CHAPTER 9
Mudslide

"What was that?" I thought to myself. A disturbing booming noise from the north end of town disrupted my concentration as I filed the accumulating paperwork associated with the lodge and mirror construction. I set up a tiny office in the back of the town council building to organize the documents and, more so, to field a steady stream of questions.

"Tia, any news on when the mirror will be delivered?" Mr. Ducey bellowed to me from the front door. He was his usual disheveled-looking self. He wasn't wearing anything that wasn't wrinkled, including the hat perched on his head that partly covered his eyes.

"Nothing new to report, Mr. Ducey. I told you I would let everyone know the minute I heard anything," I said.

"They said it would be here by today. We've been waiting for over a month. How long could it take to make a mirror?"

"I know what they said. But it's not here yet."

"Mr. Ducey, is that your mule wandering down the street?" Lorenzo asked, coming through the front door. Lorenzo, my hero! This wouldn't be the first time Lorenzo would walk in at precisely the right time and say exactly the right thing to save me. I don't think he realized how he had an uncanny way of doing that.

"Not again!" Mr. Ducey grumbled as he stumbled down the porch steps to try to catch his mule.

"Thank you!" I said with a sigh.

"For what?" Lorenzo replied.

"I didn't think he would ever leave," I said. I loved him for being my constant friend.

"There's a truckload of workers arriving despite all the rain we've been getting lately. It doesn't seem to be slowing them down. I can't believe how fast this is all happening. I wonder if they'll get the lodge completed before winter? I wouldn't think they'd be able to work past September," Loren said.

"No, I don't think so either. I wish they could get the mirror in. Everyone is anxious to see it working. I heard some people have decided to stay because of all the changes."

"Tia, where's your Pa? Or Lorenzo's? Dante Gallini yelled, out of breath, rushing through the door.

"I don't know. Why? What happened?" I asked, a bit alarmed.

"A rockslide just took out the back side of Eleanore's house. And if something doesn't happen quickly, it looks like the slide will continue taking out that whole row of homes down the street from hers," Dante replied.

"Was she inside when it happened? Is she okay?" I asked.

"Luckily, she was in the side yard feeding her chickens when it happened. Her chickens were squawking and running every which way. It would have been funny had it not been for the mud and rocks pushing over her house," Dante added.

"Tia, I'll go back with Dante. Maybe you could go find help," Lorenzo suggested.

"Ok, will do. I'll meet you up there as soon as I can," I responded. Locking up the building and stepping out onto the muddy road, I wondered where I should go first when I heard Pa's voice.

"Tia, hop in," Pa said as he pulled the reins on the horse-drawn wagon.

Luca reached out his hand and helped me into the front between him and Pa. The back of the wagon was full of men and shovels.

"I take it you heard about the rockslide," I said.

"How'd ya guess?" Luca asked slyly.

"The shovels were a dead giveaway," I said.

"Any ideas as to how to stop the mudslide?" Luca asked, looking off into the distance.

"We've got to shore up the sliding hill. This area has been a constant problem. You know how Mr. Waller and Mrs. Corner have always complained about the road being washed out? Now they've really got something to complain about," Pa said wearily.

An hour of shoveling had barely made a dent. Mud and rocks continued to cascade down the mountain. As soon as the mud was cleared, more would take its place. We were all drenched, muddy, cold, and exhausted.

"Rubin, this isn't getting us anywhere. I'm about to lose everything I've worked for my whole life!" Mr. Waller said despondently. "Do we have any logs to hold the mud in place?"

"We're doing the best we can, Ben. We'll all chip in and help rebuild your house in a better location if we can't save your home," Pa reassured.

"Are you going to rebuild ALL these houses down this row? The mud and rocks ain't going to stop at my house," Ben Waller said sarcastically.

Just then, a loud rumbling broke through the sound of shoveling, and everyone paused. Was it thunder? Was it more of the rockslide? We weren't sure if we should shovel faster or run.

When I turned toward the sound, I was dumbfounded by what I saw. Up the hill came a crane, a dump truck, a loader, one large truck full of railroad ties, and another driven by Jaden with Mr. Burton in the front and full of his workers in the back.

I watched Jaden as he got out of the truck, instructing the men what to do. I wondered if his red plaid lumberjack shirt, jeans, and high-laced boots would still be clean later on. As he pushed his thick, black-as-coal hair away from his steel-blue eyes, I surmised he often practiced that move in front of a mirror. How could someone be so appealing yet so obvious all at the same time? Thinking I'd be in big trouble if I didn't stop staring at his chiseled features, I turned just in time to see Lorenzo standing beside me.

"What do you think, Tia?" Lorenzo asked.

"About what?" I asked sharply.

"Geez, take it easy, Tia. What do you think I'm talking about? Mr. Burton saving the day...one more time?" Lorenzo responded.

"I'm sorry I snapped at you," I said, relieved he wasn't referring to my thoughts about Jaden.

"Rubin, I can put up a retaining wall to prevent any more mud sliding into these houses really quick. Would you like me to take charge of this?" Mr. Burton asked.

"That would be wonderful, Mr. Burton, but I don't know how we would repay you," Pa answered sheepishly.

"Don't have many options at this point, do you, Rubin?" Mr. Burton said glibly. "Don't worry about compensation. I see this as an investment."

"Absolutely, we want the wall!" chimed in the owners whose homes were about to be obliterated.

Mr. Burton called the foreman to go ahead and get started with the project. We all moved away to give room for the trucks. I went and stood next to Pa. He removed his hat, wiped his brow with his sleeve, ran his hands through his hair, and crossed his arms. We stared silently as Mr. Burton did what we could never have done.

The loader lifted heavy, wet dirt clods, putting them into the dump truck after cleaning up most of the rocks and mud. The crane lifted the railroad ties into place while Burton's hired hands hammered large nails through them to hold back the earth and stone.

"Mr. Burton and Jaden, you and your workers, please come to the cafe tonight for dinner on the house," Sally said.

"I'll pay for a round of drinks for the crew," Mr. Waller said.

"I'll chip in for the dessert," Mrs. Corner said.

Why, we can't thank you enough, Mr. Burton, for saving our houses. Heck, we'll pay for the meals," the rest of the owners agreed.

"Thank you, Mr. Burton, for saving our town." All of the townspeople, including Gus and Ed, cheered and clapped.

"Hey, Rubin, wasn't that incredible what Mr. Burton did?" Ben asked. "I've never seen such a thing."

"Yeah, it's something, all right," Pa softly responded, flicking the reins on the horses' backs to get them moving.

"You won't join the celebration at Sally's, Mr. Scalini?" Jaden asked.

"No, I've got other things that need my attention," Pa responded.

"What about you, Tia?" Jaden asked.

My face began to flush, and my heart pounded. I knew I needed to make a quick decision. People who mattered were watching. "I'm not sure, maybe; I'll have to see about something first," I responded.

I kicked myself for being so ambivalent. I should have just said "no." Part of me wanted to be happy for those whose houses were saved, but part of me felt so deflated. Pa and I weren't able to save our town from the freezing darkness or the rockslide, but Mr. Burton was able to do both. How could something so wonderful make me feel so bad? Maybe it was not just feeling worthless but also that nagging sense of losing my beloved town—this time to powerful people, not inclement weather.

"Hopefully, you'll get that something taken care of and join us," Jaden said.

"Oh, come on, Tia, it'll be fun. Let's go to the cafe," Lorenzo pleaded.

The feeling of defeat wouldn't let me go to the cafe. Instead, I walked home alone.

CHAPTER 10
Python or Not?

"Tia, wake up, you're yelling in your sleep, and it sounds creepy. Wake up!" Lily shouted as she shook my shoulder.

"Tia's having another nightmare?" Eileen mumbled as she put a pillow over her head to stifle the sound.

"Huh, what?" I said as I welcomed being awakened. This nightmare was similar to others where evil people were chasing me, but this one had a new twist. Throwing on my bathrobe, I stumbled down for coffee.

"You're up early," Pa said.

"Had another nightmare where I'm being chased, and then I'm in the town hall where I saw a snake slither in, and no one noticed it winding around people's legs. When it reached the podium, I realized it was a python. I watched the whole thing in the dream, but no one else noticed or cared. I wonder who the python could be?" I said.

"I have a good idea who that could be, don't you?" Pa asked.

Without even thinking, I blurted out, "Mr. Burton?"

"Bingo!" Pa replied.

"What are we going to do?" I asked.

"Nothing, yet. Your dream confirms my feelings, and so now I know we need to keep an eye on him. He may have nefarious motives for being so helpful. I really didn't like it when he said yesterday that fixing the landslide was an investment. An investment in what?" Pa said.

I saw Lorenzo through the kitchen window, heading towards us. My heart warmed as I opened the door and invited him in. "Want some coffee?"

"You bet," Lorenzo said. "You missed it last night."

"Missed what?" I asked. I handed Lorenzo the coffee in his special mug, just as he liked, with a splash of cream and a dot of sugar. He smelled of fresh-cut hay. I wondered if he'd been sleeping in the barn again. I loved that smell.

"You know we all went to the cafe last night, right? Well, some were drinking, and Mr. Burton must have had a little too much to drink. He started talking about how his father and your grandfather ran against each other for Mayor of Milan when your grandfather was young, about twenty years old."

"You mean Grandpa Rubus?" I asked.

"Yes! Anyway, Burton was saying how Rubus got caught stuffing the ballot box with fake votes. Rather than face criminal charges, he ran away. Burton's father then became the mayor of Milan, and your family was left with a blemish on their name. So, guess where your grandfather ran away to?" Lorenzo continued.

"Here?" I responded in utter dismay, visibly shaken and angered by what I had just heard.

"Yep," Lorenzo said.

"Oh my! I can't believe this!" I said, dumbfounded. "You mean he just started speaking ill of Grandpa Rubus? Tell me exactly what happened."

"Like I said, Burton seemed a little drunk and loose-lipped, unlike his usual guarded self. Anyway, he started talking about his childhood and his extremely strict father.

Everybody seemed very empathic to Burton's troubled past. He told us how he took a beating when his father thought he lost the election—before he found out about the stolen ballots. Burton put his head down for a minute. I wasn't sure what he was doing. He held his hand to his eye and the other hand below, and he pulled a glass eye out of his eye socket and held it up for all to see. We were all riveted at that point and a little disgusted.

Burton practically cried, 'This happened because of that beating, and it's all because Rubus was a lying cheat.' He went on to explain how Rubus disappeared, but not before leaving a letter stating what he had done. Rubus's confession gave Burton's father the win. But still, Burton said something to the effect of, 'He will always be a dirty thief in my mind.' There was no more party after that. Everyone patted Burton's back as they left while he sat hunched over the bar, looking like a broken man.

I was surprised everyone believed this sob story as if it were true. I didn't know what to say or do, so I hightailed it home," Lorenzo said.

Pa brushed his hands through his graying hair and stood up. "Now that man is spreading false rumors around about our founding father. Sure doesn't take long for a snake to spit out its venom, and right on my Pa's reputation. How many people do you think heard him say that, Lorenzo?" Pa asked.

"Pretty much everybody. If they didn't hear it firsthand, they'll know soon enough. You know how gossip spreads like weeds around here."

"Be ready for backlash, Tia. This will not go away on its own, especially if it's true. Warn the rest of the family what has happened. There's no telling what people will do or how they'll respond," Pa warned.

"Pa, we've got to find out the truth. How can we defend Grandpa's reputation if we don't even know if it's true or not?" I insisted.

"True or not, we all know Rubus to be an honest and forthright man. So, what if he made a mistake when he was young? Haven't we all done stupid things when we were young? He wasn't responsible for Mr. Burton's rage. Sounds to me like he did the honorable thing by leaving a letter and taking full responsibility. I wonder if Burton still has the letter. I'd sure like to see it, although that wouldn't really prove anything either because it could be a fake," Pa said.

"I'm going to visit Miss May before coming to work, Pa. Maybe she'll remember something about Grandpa being involved in this scandal," I said, hopeful.

"She's never remembered anything the other times you've visited her. What makes you think she'll remember now? Mr. Burton is going to have to come up with some proof. I'm not going to believe it just because he's got a glass eye," Pa said indignantly.

Just then, Lorenzo's dad knocked at the door. "Rubin, I thought I should come over and warn you about what happened at the cafe last night, but I see Lorenzo beat me to it. People are already asking me if what Burton said is true or not. I told them I didn't know. This could get ugly. You know how people are," Ed said.

"Yes, I know how people are. Let's meet with Gus to discuss this mess. Tia, meet us at the town hall in an hour, OK?" Pa said.

The screen door slammed after me as I headed for Miss May's.

"Miss May, can I come in?' I asked, knocking on her kitchen door. She had already opened the top half of the door, so I knew she was up. The morning mist rolled into the kitchen, mixing with the steam coming from the tea kettle, and it evoked a feeling of a mystery about to unfold.

Miss May responded, "I'm glad you're here. Can you reach into the back of that cupboard for the honey jar? Not sure how it got pushed back so far since I use some every day. What brings you over so early?"

I took down the honey, spread it on her toast, and fixed us both a cup of tea. We sat at the small wooden kitchen table, barely big enough for the two chairs that had the same floral cushions for as long as I can remember. Miss May's bottom reached over either side of the chair like peanut butter and jelly draping over both sides of the bread. Her large breasts lay atop the table, her puffy arms reaching on either side to hold the cup.

"Miss May, I know I've asked you this before, but can you remember anything about why Grandpa and Grandma came to live here in Dark Valley? Did something happen in Milan that made them leave? Wouldn't it have taken a lot for someone to stay once they realized how cold and dark it is for six months? I mean, it doesn't make sense why they would stay. Does it? Was there another reason?" I inquired.

"Now honey, let me tell you the story of how your grandpa and grandma got together. I was sharing a house with your grandma before Rubus came along. We were both schoolteachers. I taught first grade, and Ginta taught second. Rubus came back into town after being gone for a while." Miss May recounted.

"So Rubus was gone? Do you know where he went or why he was gone? How long do you think he was gone?" I asked, anxious to know all the details.

"Now, those are good questions. Hmm? As I remember, he and Ginta dated a little bit before he disappeared. Oh yes, now I remember something about Rubus running for mayor of Milan. He did something, but I'm not sure what. I didn't know Ginta then. I do vaguely remember something in the newspaper. But I really didn't pay much attention. That Burton fellow came from a very well-to-do family, and I just assumed he would win. Didn't know much about Rubus Scalini who was running against him other than he came from a nice family, just not rich like the Burtons."

"Miss May, weren't you suspicious when he showed up at your door asking to see Ginta?" I asked.

"Not really. Ginta seemed so happy to see him. I trusted her judgment. Like I said, I didn't really know them before. Plus, I thought the news could have been made up. Heck. It's not past the realm of possibilities that they lied about Rubus so Burton would win. Right?" Miss May suggested.

"I suppose you're right. How will we ever find out the truth?" I asked without expecting a reply.

"Truth is one of those things that, if you wait long enough, will surface. You will know the truth, and then you'll feel free," Miss May chuckled.

"I hope you're right, Miss May. Or maybe I don't really want to know," I said hesitantly.

"It's always best to know the truth no matter how much it hurts," Miss May encouraged.

"I better get going, Miss May. My Pa needs me to record a meeting soon," I said.

"Don't you want to hear the story of how Rubus dated and proposed to Ginta? It's a great romance story," Miss May said, insisting I stay a bit longer.

"Maybe next time," I replied, even though I'd heard that story before. "Thanks for your time, Miss May. How are your supplies holding up? We can easily get things from Milan now. Just let me know if you need anything. There are trucks bringing stuff up all the time. They're even talking about building our own supply store right in the town center. Won't that be something?" I asked.

"That is something. I can't believe how things are changing. You know Sophie checks in on me every week. I'll make a list and give it to Sophie. Thanks for stopping in. It's always a pleasure to see you, and if I think of anything else about Rubus, I'll write it down so I don't forget," Miss May said.

Her eyes sparkled like they usually did. She was so innocent, even after living for 80-some years. I always felt terrible leaving her alone, but she never seemed to mind much. *"I'm glad Sophie checks in on her. She should move in with us. Then she'd never be alone,"* I thought as I started walking to the town hall. Picking up my pace, a car slowed down right next to me. I was surprised to see Jaden rolling down the window of his red Fiat. Even with the wind blowing, not a hair was out of place. The craziest thing was that I still felt like I wanted to impress him despite my anger.

"Do you want a ride? Going to the town hall?" Jaden asked.

"I can walk just fine, thank you very much," I said curtly.

"OK, suit yourself. Look, I'm going right by the town hall. Seems kind of stupid for you to walk when you could be there in about two minutes if you'd allow yourself to take a ride. Don't worry; I don't bite."

"Never thought you did. Ok, all right," I said as I turned the handle, pulled the heavy door, and slid into the seat. I felt so awkward and nervous around him. I wasn't quite sure why. Could it be because my mistrust of his father spilled over onto him? Could it be because he was so wealthy, and I wasn't? Could it be because I had feelings for him which I didn't want to admit? Maybe a mixture of all of that.

"I guess you heard about what my dad said last night at the cafe?" Jaden said.

"Yeah, I heard about it. Seems pretty sneaky to me that he would just blurt out something so vile about my grandfather to the whole town. He's got no proof," I said.

"What about the glass eye?"

"He could have made up that whole story," I said.

"Are you calling my father a liar?" Jaden said.

"I'm just saying he's got no proof. Tell him to produce some proof. How dare he go off half-cocked and spread such a terrible story about my grandfather! My grandfather worked like a dog to make this town what it is!"

"Tia, I think it's my father who's making this town more than it's ever been," Jaden said softly as if he didn't really want to hurt my feelings.

"You can let me out right here, and I'll walk the rest of the way. Stop the car!" I almost shouted.

I had the door half open when he screeched the car to a halt. I couldn't jump out fast enough. I stomped the rest of the way. Slamming open the front door to the town hall made Pa, Ed, and Gus turn their heads to look.

"What's got into you?" Pa asked. "Tell me later. Just get your notepad and pencil so we can get this meeting started."

I found it difficult to write because my hands were shaking. And then someone else charged through the front door, which didn't help. *"Now what?"* I thought.

"I thought I'd find you three in here having one of your meetings while Mr. Burton and the rest of us are working harder than a mule team. Mr. Burton asked me to come get you three. He's up on a scaffold and needs to ask you something important," Doug insisted. "He needs you to come right away. Like I said, he's up on a scaffold."

"Ok, ok, Doug. Take it easy. We'll be right there," Pa said, running his hands through his hair. What could be so important that he would need all three of us there, and why tell Doug, the loudmouth of the town? It surprised me that Pa hadn't pulled all his hair out. I hated to see him so stressed out. "We'd better go, guys," Pa said.

"You two handle it. I've got other things I need to do. Plus, I'd hate to shake the scaffold so much that Burton falls off of it. No telling what might happen," Gus said.

"Let's just pretend we don't know about what happened in the cafe last night. Play dumb. This will give us time to figure out how we want to handle this latest news," Pa said.

"Good idea," Ed said.

"Tia, you coming?" Pa asked.

"Yep," I said.

Mr. Burton was up on the scaffold, just like Doug said. He held onto the scaffold with one hand while the other was on the large mirror. We all looked shocked, not realizing the mirror had arrived.

"Just a little adjusting and this baby is ready to go," Burton said. Rubin, do you want it facing more toward the north where it's not as sunny or the south where you can make full use of the sun or in the middle towards the town center?"

We all three said in unison, "The town center." Getting the sun for the longest time in the middle of town makes the most sense. That way, those in the north can't complain about their southern neighbors getting more sun than they do, and vice versa.

Underneath, we three were seething, knowing we had once again been tricked into a situation that elevated Burton and made us look small. It was also interesting how so much of the ski hill had already been completed and how the mirror just coincidentally was installed days before the dark season. It all seemed so staged.

When Mr. Burton climbed down from the scaffold, halfway hidden behind a post, he jerked Jaden close. He seemed very angry about something, evidently giving Jaden a tongue-lashing. I saw Jaden stiffen and his countenance fall. Feeling very sorry for him, I wished I could hear the conversation. This wasn't the first time I noticed such hostile behavior from his dad.

We all stood back, gazing at the mirror, then turned and looked down the hill toward downtown. Even on a day when sun shone in the valley, the extra sun directed toward the town hall was very noticeable. Everyone started clapping and cheering. People were slapping Mr. Burton on his back for a job well done. Meanwhile, Pa, Mr. Leone, and I stood motionless, feeling useless.

CHAPTER 11
Unraveling Memories

In celebration of the mirror being erected, this year's theme for the Octoberfest Fair would be *mirrors*. The organizers planned a special event during the festival to honor Mr. Burton with a medal and then a time for him to give a speech. I could tell Pa was even more irritated with such adulation, especially since he knew Mr. Burton did nothing that didn't benefit himself. We both were amazed at how well Mr. Burton made himself appear to be generous and caring.

"What's the matter with everyone?" Pa said one evening during dinner. "You all look like your best friend dumped you for your worst enemy."

There was no reply. We continued looking at our plates, chewing in silence. "Really, what's up? Lilly, tell me what's going on," Pa demanded.

"Our friends are avoiding us, and I can tell they are gossiping, Pa. No one will talk to us, and we don't get invited anywhere anymore. It's like we've got the plague. It all started when Mr. Burton told everyone about what Grandpa Rubus did. What can we do, Pa? It's getting really bad. I don't even like going into town because of how people treat me."

"Do you all feel this way?" Pa asked.

Everyone shook their heads yes.

"Lorenzo doesn't even come over anymore," I said sadly.

We sat silently for what seemed like a long time, no one sure of what to say.

Finally, Pa spoke, "Look, we're just going to have to ride out this storm. Mark my words: something will happen to turn this mess around. We haven't done anything but try to make this place better. We must remember who we are and what we've done for our town. Tia, don't you remember it was your discovery that started this whole mirror invention? We wouldn't be experiencing our first winter with sunlight if it weren't for us. I mean, think about it. We're the ones who found Burton and made a way for him to come up here and start this ski hill. There is nothing we can do about the gossip and vitriol except encourage one another and stick together. This will be a time for all of us to support one another."

"Pa, I'm not going to sit around and do nothing. Those Burtons are ruining our reputation on purpose. I feel like punching them. They know exactly what they're doing! It's not right!" Mica shouted.

"I agree with Mica. We've got to do something. Maybe we could have a town hall meeting and set the record straight," Luca said.

"And what good would that do? We don't even know what is true. It might just make us look more guilty," Pa said. "I say we keep our mouths shut for now. Burton eventually will show his true colors."

CHAPTER 11
Unraveling Memories

In celebration of the mirror being erected, this year's theme for the Octoberfest Fair would be *mirrors*. The organizers planned a special event during the festival to honor Mr. Burton with a medal and then a time for him to give a speech. I could tell Pa was even more irritated with such adulation, especially since he knew Mr. Burton did nothing that didn't benefit himself. We both were amazed at how well Mr. Burton made himself appear to be generous and caring.

"What's the matter with everyone?" Pa said one evening during dinner. "You all look like your best friend dumped you for your worst enemy."

There was no reply. We continued looking at our plates, chewing in silence. "Really, what's up? Lilly, tell me what's going on," Pa demanded.

"Our friends are avoiding us, and I can tell they are gossiping, Pa. No one will talk to us, and we don't get invited anywhere anymore. It's like we've got the plague. It all started when Mr. Burton told everyone about what Grandpa Rubus did. What can we do, Pa? It's getting really bad. I don't even like going into town because of how people treat me."

"Do you all feel this way?" Pa asked.

Everyone shook their heads yes.

"Lorenzo doesn't even come over anymore," I said sadly.

We sat silently for what seemed like a long time, no one sure of what to say.

Finally, Pa spoke, "Look, we're just going to have to ride out this storm. Mark my words: something will happen to turn this mess around. We haven't done anything but try to make this place better. We must remember who we are and what we've done for our town. Tia, don't you remember it was your discovery that started this whole mirror invention? We wouldn't be experiencing our first winter with sunlight if it weren't for us. I mean, think about it. We're the ones who found Burton and made a way for him to come up here and start this ski hill. There is nothing we can do about the gossip and vitriol except encourage one another and stick together. This will be a time for all of us to support one another."

"Pa, I'm not going to sit around and do nothing. Those Burtons are ruining our reputation on purpose. I feel like punching them. They know exactly what they're doing! It's not right!" Mica shouted.

"I agree with Mica. We've got to do something. Maybe we could have a town hall meeting and set the record straight," Luca said.

"And what good would that do? We don't even know what is true. It might just make us look more guilty," Pa said. "I say we keep our mouths shut for now. Burton eventually will show his true colors."

"But maybe not before he takes over our town and ruins it," Luca said. "I wouldn't put it past him to run for mayor and take your place, Pa."

"Papa, Octoberfest is going to be ruined because of this. It's usually my favorite time of year. Lilly's been working so hard all year on her quilt. I've got a new little lamb to show at the stock show, and Eileen's planning on winning the peach pie prize. But now it's all ruined!" Sophie sobbed.

"There're two weeks before the fair. A lot can happen in two weeks. We'll have fun like we always do; hopefully, people will forget all about Grandpa Rubus."

"Sophie, do you think Miss May can make it to the fair this year?" I asked.

"I don't know. It's getting harder for her to walk," Sophie replied.

"What if we provide her a ride to the fair and just let her sit, and we'll all take turns keeping an eye on her?" I questioned.

"Why? What's so important about her being there?" Sophie asked.

"I don't like her being alone so much. It will be good for her to get out. And maybe being around people will jog some memories," I answered.

The committee did an excellent job decorating downtown with banners, garlands, pumpkins, squash, hay bales, and mirrors. There were mirrors everywhere. Mirrors hung in the least expected places, like in between hay bales and along with the banners and garlands. There were mirrors at stop signs. They even created a maze of mirrors as one of the fun activities. There was a thick feeling of hope and joy in the air.

We cascaded into Miss May's kitchen and asked, "Are you ready, Miss May, to go to the fair?"

"Fair? Oh, is that today? I thought that was next week," Miss May replied. "It will only take me a minute to get ready."

"Let me help you," I said as I put my hand around her plump arm and my other arm under her other armpit, pushing her to her feet.

"I want to wear my new flowered dress I got from Milan," Miss May said. "It will match my orange sweater so perfectly. I'm so excited to wear it today. This is such a treat for all of you to come and fetch me."

"Oh, no, Miss May, we are so glad you are coming. We're just sorry we didn't think of it long ago," Sophie said. "Let me help you with your stockings while Tia helps you with your dress, and Lilly will do your hair while Eileen does your makeup."

We were a whirlwind of motion, moving Miss May's arms and legs as if she were a rag doll getting dressed. Sophie rolled the stockings up Miss May's legs. At the same time, I slid the dress over her head, guiding one arm through the sleeve and then the other. Afterward, Lily did a fantastic job curling Miss May's straight hair. After powder, rouge, and a swipe of lipstick, Miss May looked better than I had ever seen her. She was practically a new woman. I carefully held the orange sweater for her to push her arms through to finish off the autumn outfit.

"Oops, I almost forgot my purse," Miss May announced. "Be a dear, Sophie, and fetch it from the bedroom dresser."

"We're going in Mr. Leone's car," I said as we headed out the front door.

"Oh, my, I've never been in a car before!" Miss May exclaimed. "Are you sure it's safe?"

"It's as safe as riding in a buggy and a lot more fun," Lily said.

"So, put your derriere in first," I said as I opened the front door for her.

Her large backside almost didn't fit into the front bench but landed as if accidentally on the cloth seat. I bent down and put my hands around her even plumper ankles, turning her whole body into the car. We all giggled along with Miss May at the sight of her being put in the car. The giggles continued as Lily drove down her lane toward town with the rest of us in the back seat. I felt such an atmosphere of sisterly love at that moment.

The festivities were well underway by the time we arrived. We set up Miss May in the town square where all the speech giving and pomp and circumstance would be happening around 3 pm. I took the first shift to stay with Miss May while the others went to set up their entries for the competitions. I could see most of the booths from our vantage point in the park since they were all arranged in a circle around the promenade.

"What's that bell ringing, Tia?" Miss May wondered.

"That's the muscle booth where people pay a penny to hit this wedge of wood with a sledgehammer. If they hit it hard enough, it pushes a piece of metal covered with wood up this long post and hits the bell. Doug and Dougy Duce are running it. Do you remember them?" I asked.

"I don't recall. What do they look like?"

"Mr. Duce is a big man with huge muscles and a mouth to match. Dougy is a smaller version. They have a pig farm, and Doug does odds and ends for people, including any kind of fix-it project. But they only arrived a few years ago, so you may not have met them," I informed.

"What are some of the other booths," Miss May asked, squinting in several directions. "My eyes aren't as good as they used to be."

"There is the ball toss. The objective is to try to knock down the gadget with a ball. Then there is the hoop toss, where you throw a small wooden hoop that looks like a cross-stitch frame and try to snag it over a long-necked bottle," I said.

"Oh, I remember those; we used to have fairs like this in Milan. I remember going to one just like this one when I was young," Miss May said, reminiscing.

With Miss May talking in the background, my attention was drawn to Lorenzo and his buddies going from booth to booth. I wondered if he was purposefully avoiding eye contact with me. I figured he was since he hadn't been by the house in so long. Lorenzo and his friends were tossing a ball back and forth to each other and kicking it up in the air. They weren't paying attention to where they were going and ran into me.

"Hey, watch out!" I shouted, almost being knocked over.

"Sorry, sorry, we didn't mean anything by it. Just horsing around," Lorenzo said. He stopped, shocked, when he realized it was me.

"Come on, Lorenzo, let's go check out the muscle man booth," Lorenzo's brother said.

Off they went, leaving me speechless and feeling like yesterday's leftovers. "I can't believe Lorenzo treated me like that. How dare he totally ignore me like I'm a piece of furniture!" I lamented.

"Tia, don't let those boys get under your skin. They're just showing off in front of each other. You know how stupid young boys can be," Miss May said. "Why don't you go get us a drink from one of those booths? I've heard of a new drink called Coca-Cola, and I'd like to try it. Wouldn't you?" Miss May said as she pulled a lira from her purse.

"I've already tried it, but I would love to have one right now. Good idea, Miss May," I said as I headed to the nearest booth.

Jaden was standing near the drink booth. He said, "What's eating you?"

"Nothing, none of your business," I replied as I stood in line.

"I'll have two Coca-Colas, please," I told the vendor, trying to ignore Jaden.

No sooner did I try to hand the lira to the vendor than Jaden handed him *his* lira, ordering another for himself, too.

"Thank you," is all I could think to say.

"You're welcome," Jaden said.

For a moment, all my defenses were gone.

"Would you like to come and sit with Miss May and myself, or are you too busy?" I asked.

"Sure, I have a few free minutes to meet your aunt," Jaden said.

"She's not my aunt. She was good friends with my Grandma Ginta and Grandpa Rubus—the one your father said was a cheat and a liar," I added.

"Jeez, Tia, don't you ever take a break?" Jaden said.

"Sorry, but the whole town is treating me like a leper since your father spread that story. Don't you remember that my father and I are the ones who started this whole thing? You wouldn't even be here if it weren't for us," I snapped. I immediately felt stupid for saying the last part.

"Look, I don't think it's a big deal one way or the other. Why is everyone making such a big deal about it?" Jaden said.

"It is a big deal to me and my whole family. We don't take lightly when someone calls anyone in our family a liar and a cheat. And the town knows it's a big deal, too. They've trusted us to run this town since its inception, and now you're telling them they should never have trusted us. I'm sorry we ever asked you to come and help us. It has turned into a total disaster for my family. I don't know why you don't understand that," I said, almost crying.

"I'm sorry, Tia. Really, I am," Jaden said as he reached for my hand and lightly squeezed it.

"Jaden, what are you doing?" Mr. Burton shouted from his car. "We need to get to the stage for our presentation."

Jaden let Tia's hand go reluctantly. Looking into his blue eyes melted my heart. He seemed to be genuinely sorry for the whole mess. He stood staring into my eyes for the longest time, and I wished he didn't have to go. My heart was fluttering like a mob of butterflies.

"Tia, that boy likes you," Miss May said. "I can tell from the way he looks at you."

"I don't know, Miss May. I don't know anything anymore," I said. We sat silently, sipping our drinks as we watched the field and the square fill with people.

Everyone wandered over, and together, we braced ourselves for Burton's speech. We did not know what to expect when an unfamiliar voice came over the loudspeaker.

"Tia Scalini, Tia Scalini, please come to the stage right away. Calling Tia Scalini to the stage."

We all looked at each other wide-eyed. *"What could this be about?"* I wondered.

Pa said, "You better go, Tia; they're calling you."

As I walked toward the stage, I saw Jaden looking for me. He waved me to come quickly when he saw me in the distance.

"What's up?" I asked.

"Look, my dad and I want you to say a few words, too, since you're the one who discovered the idea of the mirror. You're right; none of this would be happening without you and your Pa."

Immediately, they started announcing the winners of all the competitions. Lily won second place for her quilt. Eileen won runner-up for her pie, and Sophie won first place for her lamb.

Before I knew it, Mr. Burton was giving his speech. It was full of platitudes for all the townspeople and workers who had contributed to the installation of the mirror. I thought Pa should be the one to give the speech instead of me, but everything happened so fast. I found myself in front of the microphone with little time to frame a speech, which may have been a good thing.

"Keep it simple, sweet, and short," I told myself. "Thank you for the opportunity to say a few words. First, I do thank Mr. Burton for everything he's done so far to make this moment possible. As we all know, it takes a special kind of person to live in a place where it's dark for six months of the year. And we all know many people have chosen to leave. So, with this mirror, we expect our town to flourish. I'd also like to thank my Pa, Gus Greco, and Ed Leone, who

have been so instrumental in making the mirror a reality. But mostly, I thank my grandfather, Rubus Scalini, for his foresight and vision to establish our town. It takes a strong and resolute man like my grandfather to settle in this beautiful valley atop this mountain. Who would have thought this most exquisite place would one day be home to so many wonderful people? I hope we can remember all the ways he has blessed our town. We wouldn't be here if it weren't for him. Thank you."

A few claps were coming from my family, but then I saw others clapping, starting with Jaden and spreading. He came over and shook my hand. Meanwhile, Mr. Burton glared at me to show his disapproval of my speech. Jaden stopped shaking my hand immediately when he saw his father's expression. Jaden backed away as I walked down the stairs off the stage.

I met back up with my family, and they all congratulated me for my speech. Miss May spoke up and said unexpectedly, "Tia, you know how you asked me the other day if I remember anything about Rubus' life before marrying your grandma? Well, when Mr. Burton was talking just now, it reminded me of his father, who gave his acceptance speech as the mayor of Milan many years ago. He mentioned Rubus and how he stole ballots or stuffed the ballot boxes. I do remember there being a big to-do and then the disappearance of Rubus. He never really showed his face in town again except when he proposed to Ginta," Miss May recounted.

We all stood there dumbfounded.

"Oh dear, I see I've upset you all. Maybe I shouldn't have told you that. From my perspective, Rubus was always an honest, hardworking man who felt bad about his mistake and spent his whole life making up for that one bad choice. You all should be proud of your grandfather. You're right, Tia, when you said he was strong and resolute. Actually, I often wondered why he went overboard to make sure he told the absolute truth."

"Thank you, Miss May, for being honest. At least now we know, and we can move on. That really helps to answer so many questions about why Rubus and Ginta chose to stay and have their family here. I guess they made good out of something bad. We have much to learn from them in so many ways, right gang?" Pa said.

A sudden whirlwind hitting a pile of autumn leaves mirrored my feelings. I blurted, "How could Mr. Burton do so many good things and yet be so shady in his motives? How could today be so wonderful and so difficult all at the same time? How could I feel so good about my speech but feel so bad about the news we just learned about Rubus? How could something so good, like the mirror, turn into something so bad that tainted our reputation?"

"I think we are all feeling some of those emotions, Tia. I guess you're learning how life is never just one thing. It's a mixture of so many things, good and bad," Pa said.

CHAPTER 12
Now What?

The sounds of ski lodge construction reverberated throughout the town like a bird pecking a metal stove pipe. Despite dropping temperatures and snowflakes, production continued. Many of the workers came up from Milan during the weekdays, stayed in large camp tents, and returned to their homes on the weekend. The lodge was halfway complete, settled near the base of the ski hill. Workers were also felling giant trees to clear the ski runs for the coming season. Burton was aiming for a February opening, even though it was unlikely.

This Tuesday in January was especially busy at the town hall office, where I was now spending most of my days fielding questions and managing day-to-day issues that were constantly coming up. Like one of many days, Jaden stopped by with questions and small talk.

"Hey Tia, how's it going?" Jaden asked.

"Pretty busy, how about you?" I replied.

"You wouldn't happen to have a pencil I could borrow?" he said.

"Borrow, or do you mean to keep, lose, or break like so many items you've taken?" I replied jokingly.

"It's not like I've stolen anything. I've asked for everything I've taken," Jaden said laughingly.

"I'm kind of glad you're such a clutz; it gives me a chance to see you more often," I said.

"So, you're getting used to my visits? Maybe I shouldn't come so often. You know what they say. Absence makes the heart grow fonder," Jaden poked.

"Here you go," I said. As I passed the pencil to Jaden, our hands touched, and he made certain his touch lasted longer than needed. Later that day, I ordered a box of pencils just for Jaden's return visits.

"Thanks, Tia. Don't know what I would do without you," Jaden said as he headed for the door.

"You're not going to stay for a cup of coffee?"

"Not today. Some friends have come up from Milan, and we're going skiing. Father wants me to try out the new pulley system to see if it's working properly. Should be good with all the new snow last night," Jaden said.

"Have fun!"

"Thanks. Maybe we could go for drinks later at Sally's?" Jaden asked.

"Sounds good; swing by on your way out," I replied.

About an hour later, booms erupted from the ski hill, which was not that uncommon. Often, dynamite was detonated to flatten the ski hill. But this hadn't happened in a while, and this one seemed different, shaking the town hall. I continued working, telling myself it must just be another prescribed explosion, until I heard the front door slam. I looked up to see Lorenzo standing there, out of breath.

Not knowing what to think or say, I just sat there while Lorenzo sputtered, "There's been an explosion, and people are hurt!"

"What happened?" I exclaimed.

"I'm not sure, but it looks like something exploded and started a fire in the lodge, which also set off an avalanche on the ski hill," Lorenzo answered.

"Oh, mio Dio! Jaden and his friends went skiing today. They may have gotten caught in the avalanche," I shouted, putting my hands over my mouth in shock.

"Many people were skiing today because of the fresh snowfall last night. That was the first snow we'd had in a few weeks after a warm spell. The snow underneath wasn't steady, creating perfect conditions for an avalanche," Lorenzo added.

Our volunteer fire truck brigade screamed by the hall on its way to put out the fire. This conversation was one of a few times Lorenzo and I had spoken since Grandpa Rubus' reputation had been smeared. While time seemed to have made all that a distant memory in people's minds. It was just so confusing to have Lorenzo turn on me then and be so nice now.

It felt good to talk to him again, however. "What are you going to do now?" I asked.

"Mr. Burton is asking for volunteers to hunt for the skiers in the snow. He said we need as many as possible, and time is of the essence. We need to find them before they suffocate," Lorenzo said. "Do you have a long pole or stick to help search?"

Lorenzo gazed into my eyes like he used to do. I looked down, not knowing what to think after his long silence.

"It's so good to talk to you again," Lorenzo said. "I've missed you. I'm sorry I've been such an idiot lately."

"What happened to you? You hurt my feelings by being so distant. Not sure what I did to make you ignore me," I said.

"My buddies, now ex-buddies, were influencing me to avoid you because of what Mr. Burton said about your grandfather. I told them to take a hike. I hope you can forgive me," Lorenzo said apologetically.

"Of course, I forgive you. I'm just unsure if I can count on you to really be my friend," I said. "I guess time will tell."

"Tell me how I can make it up to you," Lorenzo said.

"You better go help find the buried skiers before it's too late. This conversation can wait," I insisted. "I'll come up as soon as I can to be a part of the search and rescue team."

"OK, but hurry," Lorenzo said, gazing again into my eyes. He held my hand for the longest time. Those old, warm, mushy feelings came flooding back.

"Go!" I said, pushing his arm away.

When I finally got up to the hill, I saw the firefighters had put out most of the fire, which had ruined a good portion of the new construction. The injured were being helped into vehicles and taken to the town hall, where the town doctor was waiting to care for them.

I joined the row of volunteers hunting for the skiers as they slowly walked up the ski hill with long poles, gently jabbing the snow while feeling for bodies underneath. We were instructed to be as quiet as possible and listen for any sounds coming from underneath the snow. More of the townspeople started gathering with reports of missing family members. Among the missing were Jaden and his friends. Mr. Burton organized the rescue teams. He explained how there wasn't much time before pockets of trapped air beneath the fallen snow would run out of oxygen, and those pockets of air could be keeping the buried skiers alive.

Shortly after starting, Mr. Burton found Jaden and his friends. It didn't take much to pull them out, since they were are the edge of the snowslide. Others hurried to assist them to the makeshift triage station.

As Mr. Burton was aiding Jaden, he seemed to purposefully pass by Pa and me to say, "Whoever did this is going to pay a high price for almost killing my son."

More people arrived as the news spread. The searchers walked very slowly in a row only a shoulder-width apart. Luckily, the avalanche area wasn't too expansive, so walking it wouldn't take long.

As we were searching, one of the missing skiers actually came skiing down the mountain. Harry had been hiking above the avalanche area and had missed the whole thing. He joined in the search.

Now, there were only three to find. The search team walked slowly as they poked long poles into the deep snow. If the poles struck something, we called "halt," so everyone stopped. The diggers then came in behind us to see if there was a person below as the line of pokers continued on.

Allison Cook yelled, "Halt!"

Quickly, volunteers came with shovels, digging right where she felt something with her pole. The line continued to move forward slowly.

Henry Stuple yelled, "I found an arm and a head!"

Several others joined in to help Henry pull out the buried person, who turned out to be Murphy Scalia.

"Hey everybody, we found Murphy. Bring the stretcher up here!" Henry shouted.

Murphy was gasping for air, gulping it in like a thirsty puppy. They tried to lay him on a stretcher, which the EMTs brought, but Murphy would have none of that.

Murphy said, "I'm fine, I'm fine. You may need this stretcher for someone else. I was skiing with Kate and Fergie right behind me. I'm sure they are buried nearby."

No sooner had he finished his sentence than another searcher yelled, "I feel something!" The fourth person down the row also yelled, "I do, too!" Everyone set to work immediately, not waiting for the diggers. They knew time was running out for these poor souls. The ambulance driver tried to get as close as possible to the activity.

"I can hear a voice. It might be Kate. She's talking to me. She must be in an air pocket," hollered a volunteer.

People were speedily burrowing through the snow with their hands, pushing the snow out of the hole as fast as they could. Some almost fell headlong into the hole. Finally, a hand, an arm, and then the whole of Kate came through. She was cold and shaken, shivering violently.

One more, just one more person to go. Everyone then dug frantically in the final location, trying to get closer to the buried person, but this was taking longer than the others. Some were getting discouraged, thinking that maybe the location was wrong or, even worse—that it was too late.

Kate shouted, "Fergie was right next to me! I know it's him; keep searching!"

This gave them renewed hope, and they continued. Finally, they found Fergie unconscious, barely breathing. Pulling him from the snow, they immediately gave him a warm blanket and rushed him off in the ambulance to Milan. Luckily, the Milan ambulance was there within a very short time of the accident. I wondered how they arrived so quickly.

Some volunteers lay exhausted in the snow for a minute. Some cried, some cheered, and some just stared into space. This was the worst catastrophe ever to have happened in the valley. Pa and I went to the town hall to see how things were going. Plus, I wanted to see Jaden. I could give him some hot chocolate, thinking that might cheer him up, but when we got there, he was already gone. That's odd. I thought he would have been there for at least a couple of hours. The idea of visiting him at his house was only a fleeting thought. There was no way I would go to his home after what his father said.

"Pa, you weren't near the fire or explosions when they happened, were you? Do you know how they got started?" I asked.

"No, I was working in our garage," Pa said. "I ran toward the sound of the boom when I heard it from home."

"Did you call the Milan ambulance about the accident?"

"No, I didn't even know what was happening," Pa replied. "Why do you ask?"

"I don't know how the ambulances would have arrived so quickly. Just seems strange," I said.

CHAPTER 13
The Investigation

"Pa, Pa!" I called from the yard into the barn. Stopping to catch my breath, I continued, "Pa, there are two men from Milan at the front door. They say they're investigators wanting to talk with you about the ski hill accident."

"Well, did you invite them in?" Pa asked.

"No, I got scared. Why do they want to talk to you?"

"I don't know. Let's go find out," Pa replied. We walked from the barn through the snow back to the house.

"Hello, gentlemen, come on in. I'd shake your hands, but I don't suppose you'd like grease from my carburetor on your nice, clean hands," Pa said.

They all shuffled into the little kitchen. The two men's heads almost reached the ceiling. They took off their hats, which helped a little. I must have been staring at them because one man cleared his throat several times, shifting from one foot to another.

"Have a seat at the table," Pa invited them while he went to the kitchen sink.

Pa pumped the handle to the spigot until water came pouring out. The squeaking of the rusty handle and Jeb's intimidating snarls added more tension to the already stressful situation. Grabbing a bar of Eileen's lye and lavender soap, he seemed to take his time washing his hands. I wondered if he was purposfully delaying the meeting to calm his nerves or to irritate the guests? I felt the stern looks of the investigators practically searing holes into Pa's back and knew it would take more than a squeaky pump and a growling dog to make them leave.

"Would you like some tea? Scones were made fresh this morning. Would you like one?" Pa asked.

"Mr. Scalini, we have some questions about last week's ski hill explosion. This isn't a social visit. My name is Inspector Phillips. This is my associate, Mr. Reed."

"Yes, wonderful to meet you. I'm afraid I don't have much to say, gentlemen. I was nowhere near the accident when it happened," Pa said.

"Is this your glove, Mr. Scalini?" Inspector Phillips asked. He held up a black, well-worn, slightly singed glove.

"Well, what do you know, I've been looking all over for that," Rubin said.

"Don't you want to know where we found the glove, Mr. Scalini?" Mr. Phillips asked.

"Call me Rubin, Mr. Phillips. We're not too formal around these parts. I think you're about to tell me where you found the glove, whether I want to know or not," Pa retorted.

I stood frozen like a Greek statue, watching Pa get fileted like a fish.

"We found this glove near the furnace that blew up. Someone started the fire, which ignited the furnace and burst the propane tank, starting the avalanche that almost killed several people. Whoever started that fire is mighty lucky no one died." Mr. Phillips said. "Where were you when the explosion happened, Mr. Scalini?"

"I was in my garage working on the carburetor of my truck," Pa responded.

"Did anyone see you during that time, Mr. Scalini?" Mr. Phillips asked.

"No, everyone was busy that morning," Pa said.

"You mean to tell me you have seven children, and not one was home that morning?" Mr. Phillip asked again.

"Don't you think that's mighty peculiar, Mr. Reed? Seven kids and no one can vouch for their Pa's whereabouts," Mr. Phillips said.

Mr. Reed shook his head up and down like an owl on a grandfather clock at noon.

"Mr. Phillips, I was working at the town hall, like most mornings. Luca and Mica were working at the lodge. Sophie and Tommy were tending the sheep. Lily and Eileen were cleaning Miss May's house. It's not at all unusual for no one to be home because we are a very industrious family. It would be more unusual for someone to *be* home, actually, Mr. Phillips," I declared.

"Miss Scalini, I am talking with your father and would appreciate your being quiet," Mr. Phillips said coarsely.

I crossed my arms and scowled like an angry dog.

"Tia, please go upstairs, and take Jeb with you," Pa directed.

Pulling on Jeb's collar, I dragged him, growling all the way to the steps. Then, seeing Jeb's favorite fetching ball on the floor, I threw it to the top step. I followed as Jeb chased it, leaving the kitchen quiet in our absence. I perched myself resolutely at the top of the steps, hoping to listen while petting Jeb to keep him quiet as he settled under my arm.

"So, Luca and Mica work at the lodge? Did either of them get hurt from the explosion, Mr. Scalini?" Mr. Phillips inquired.

"No, they are both fine," Pa said.

"Why didn't they get hurt?" Mr. Phillips asked.

"I think they've been working at the other end of the lodge lately," Pa said.

"That's convenient," Mr. Phillips said with evident suspicion.

"Convenient? What are you talking about?" Pa responded incredulously.

"That will be all for now, Mr. Scalini. We'll be in touch," Mr. Phillips said as he rose, extending his hand to shake Pa's hand and leaving quickly.

That night at dinner, Luca and Mica recounted how Mr. Reed and Mr. Phillips interrogated them.

Luca started, "They first separated us. Mr. Reed interrogated me, and Mr. Phillips talked to Mica. Mr. Reed asked me about how the fire didn't hurt me in an accusatory tone like I somehow knew the fire would happen, as if we knew where to work to avoid it. I was so offended. He was actually implying that you, Pa, had purposefully told us to work at the other end of the lodge to avoid getting caught in the fire. Although, I did say that you suggested that we try to get the job at this end because we would be inside where it's shielded from the weather. It was so crazy. Then they asked if you'd been up to the lodge that day, and we both told how you had brought us lunch since we were running late."

"Like that's a big deal?" Mica added.

"It does put me at the crime scene the day of the fire. That can't be a good thing," Pa said.

Luca continued, "As they left, I overheard them discussing how those two things were not enough to develop a case. Mr. Phillips went on to say that Mr. Burton swears Pa did it because Pa and the town board never wanted the ski lodge, just the mirror. That you had agreed to those things in order to get the mirror. Once the mirror was in place, you tried sabotaging the work on the ski operation. Which is ridiculous, we all know. The other guy, Mr. Reed, disagreed with Mr. Phillips, saying that these factors were insufficient to build a case. But get this. Mr. Phillips then admits the real reason for pursuing the case. He said that Burton could fire him, and he can't afford to lose his job."

Pa got up from the table, running his hand through his hair as we all sat silently, not knowing what to say. Nobody felt like eating after that, and as we cleaned the kitchen, we heard a knock at the kitchen door.

"Hi Lily, is your Pa home? I need to speak with him for a minute. I know it's late, but I'll only be a minute," Ed said, standing in the dark.

"Of course, come in. Pa's in the living room," Lily responded as we all corralled into the living room.

"Ed, what brings you over this late in the day? Are there any new developments in the explosion case? There were two investigators over here today asking me questions. I told them I didn't know anything about it. How come you're not handling the investigation?" Pa asked.

"Burton said it was only fair that we bring in outside investigators since the explosion happened on his private property outside of Dark Valley's limits. He brought in these two, who were the closest investigators. Mr. Phillips asked me if he could use the sheriff's office to interrogate you tomorrow. I had to give him permission. It was either that or he would have to drive you to Milan, and I didn't think that was a very good option. What's this nonsense about your glove being found near the propane tank?" Ed asked.

"They said it's my glove, and it sure looks like the one I'm missing. But it could be any one of a hundred gloves that look just the same. It's going to be a mighty short interrogation because I've got nothing to say," Pa said.

"Be careful, Rubin. They are probably experts at twisting words. Do you want me to find you a lawyer?"

"I can't afford a lawyer; you know that, Ed," Pa said. "I'll be telling the truth, so I'm sure it will all work out fine," Pa continued.

I followed Pa the next morning, far enough behind so he wouldn't see me. Crouching underneath the window to the interrogation room, I was able to hear the whole conversation.

"Starting time 8 a.m.," Mr. Phillips said as he recorded it in his log. "Mr. Scalini, please tell us your full name, address, and age."

"Rubin Joseph Scalini, 12 Scalini Way, Dark Valley, 45 years old."

"Where were you the day of the ski lodge explosion and avalanche, February 2, 1910? Please explain everything you did leading up to the explosion," Mr. Phillips said.

"I got up about 6 a.m., drank coffee, and then went into the barn and worked on the carburetor in the truck. I was trying to fix it rather than replace it. The boys asked me if I could bring them lunch since they were running late, so I brought them lunch around 10 a.m. and then came right back to continue work on the truck. I was there until I heard the booming sound, at which time I went to the town hall first and then to the ski hill," Rubin responded.

"It puts you at the scene of the crime that morning. Isn't it also true that you suggested to your sons that they work on the other end of the building where most of the outside construction was finished, which would be the farthest from the area where the explosion happened?" Mr. Phillips asked.

"Well, yes, but..." Pa said.

"Isn't it true you told your sons to work where there was no chance of them being harmed when you started the fire? Isn't that right?" Mr. Phillips grilled. "Isn't it also true, Mr. Scalini, that you never wanted that ski lodge built in the first place?"

"No, that's not true. I just thought it was rather frivolous, and well, I did think it would totally change the atmosphere of our town. It would make us a recreation town rather than a farm and family-friendly town," Rubin said.

"Isn't it also true that you've done everything possible to fight Mr. Burton from doing his work and completing the ski lodge and hill?" Mr. Phillips accused.

My legs started aching from squatting so long, and I had the bright idea to bring them some food to give Pa moral support. I ran home, fixed a couple of sandwiches, and quickly returned. I heard loud voices in the interrogation room, and by the looks of Mr. Leone's expression, I knew things were not going any better. "Mr. Leone, would it be possible to interrupt the meeting to see if they need some water or lunch or something?" I asked.

"No way, I can't stop an ongoing interrogation."

"Well, if you won't, I will," I insisted. Quickly opening the door, my throat was in my stomach when I saw Pa hunched over the table.

"Excuse me, Mr. Phillips, I've brought some lunch for you two in case you'd like a break," I said.

The smell of cigarettes and sweat hit me in the face. The single table and low light in an otherwise barren room gave one a sense of hopelessness. A small window covered in bars did nothing to improve the feeling.

"Miss Scalini, you have no right to disrupt this meeting; get out!" Mr. Phillips barked.

Pa perked up when he saw me and winked at me as I stepped backward out the door. My heart sank with the realization that we were in deep trouble. With the town hall right next to the sheriff's office, I easily checked in every hour. I went back at about 7 p.m., thinking for sure Pa would be released by then, but instead, I was met with the most dichotomous sight I'd ever seen—Pa in handcuffs. Hearing the bars lock with Pa inside took my breath away. I put my hand over my mouth in disbelief.

"We'll have an arraignment for Mr. Scalini as soon as we can get a judge up from Milan," Mr. Reed said. "Until then, Mr. Scalini will remain in jail. Is that clear, Mr. Leone?"

I couldn't contain myself for another second. "Pa, what's going on? How can they just put you in jail?" I gasped, clinging to the bars, trying to get as close to Pa as possible.

"Is this really necessary?" Ed asked. "Rubin's home is here; there's no chance of him running."

"We'll let the judge from Milan decide that. He'll be up in a couple of days," Mr. Phillips snapped.

"Mr. Leone, I'll get some dinner for you and Pa and be right back," I said.

"I don't have much of an appetite," Pa said.

"I'll bring a pillow and a blanket, too, Pa, so maybe you can sleep." Running home in tears, I encountered Lorenzo, who happened to be in our front yard.

Reaching out to catch me, Lorenzo said, "I just came over to check on things. What's the matter, Tia?"

The kindness of his gesture turned my tears to sobs as I fell into his strong arms.

"Tia, tell me what happened!" Lorenzo yelled in my face as he held it firmly between his rough hands. "But can we go inside? It's freezing out here."

In between sobs, catching my breath, hiccups, and blowing my nose, I managed to explain everything to everyone. Amidst sighs, gasps, and tears, I told the heart-wrenching story. When I had finished, there was no sound except for Sophie's muffled sobs.

"Oh no, I forgot I promised to bring them dinner!" I jumped to my feet.

We all scurried to pack up the leftovers and Pa's favorites, including his slippers, a pillow, and a comforter. Like a troop of army volunteers, we marched back to the jail with bundles of goodies, including pillows and blankets for everyone.

"It was Sophie's idea, and we all thought it was great," I said as we nestled down to sleep in the jailhouse with Pa.

We couldn't imagine being home in our comfortable beds while Pa slept on an old cot. Soon, there was the familiar sound of Jeb snoring next to me as I dozed off into a night of fitful sleep.

CHAPTER 14
The Stinging Truth

The judge released Pa under his own recognizance with the trial set to occur in three months. Pa's public defender, Mr. Chambers from Milan, said the prosecution was very flimsy, and he couldn't imagine a jury finding Pa guilty.

"I'm actually surprised it's going to trial," Mr. Chambers said. "But I suppose the judge knows Mr. Burton, and he too might be afraid of losing his job, so he will do what he's told."

I said to Lorenzo one evening, "I don't feel good about how the defense is going. Mr. Chambers is not investigating to find the real criminal. He just says the prosecution's evidence is flimsy, that they have no case. But what if Mr. Burton bribes the jury, too? The only way we can ensure a fair trial for Pa is to find out who really did it."

"What are you going to do?" Lorenzo asked.

"I was hoping we could start asking people what they heard or saw on the day of the explosion. It wouldn't have to be like an interrogation, just a normal conversation. That way, people won't be suspicious," I said.

"You're including me on this secret mission?" Lorenzo said with a smile.

"Yes, and my whole family. Everyone thought it would be a good idea, especially Luca and Mica since they work on the ski hill," I added.

"Count me in because I just got a job up there, too," Lorenzo said.

"Thanks, we need as many ears as possible," I said, giving him a peck on his cheek. "You're the best."

"That's all I get?" Lorenzo said, pulling me close. I didn't object as he gave me a clumsy kiss on the lips. "I'm so glad we're back together, Tia. I'm sorry I believed all the gossip about your grandpa and your family," Lorenzo said.

"You can make it up to me by helping me find out who *really* set the fire. I'd better go," I said, not wanting to leave.

Winter always seemed to be a time of waiting, but even more so this year as we watched and listened for even a smidge of evidence to exonerate Pa. To keep ourselves distracted from the tension of the ongoing case, we got the notion that it would be fun to cross country ski on moonlit nights. Since we had no skis nor money to buy them, we thought why not just make them ourselves.

Of course, Tommy was the one to engineer them. He knew we needed to collect the wood from the many felled pine trees in the forest. Lodgepoles seemed to work the best, being lightweight enough to easily be transported back to the barn. By the light of the gas lantern, Tommy first shaved off the bark. He'd throw the useless wood into the furnace to keep it running strong so we didn't freeze. Then he cut the trunk into long chunks which, when shaved and sanded, took on the appearance of skis.

Once they were the right shape, he'd then show us how to wax the bottom to make it slippery in the snow. My arm ached from layering on the wax made from hog fat. The more layers the better the ride, we surmised.

Finally, he nailed a strap on the sides to slide our feet into, adding a wedge piece to stop our feet from sliding too far forward.

While we were busy with the skis, Tommy showed Luca and Mica how to make the poles. Fresher logs worked best because they were bendable yet firm but not so firm that they would easily break. Once they found the right aged wood, it took hours to whittle it into shape. A pointed bottom and a leather strap at the top completed the homemade poles.

It was just the five of us youngest ones who worked in the ski assembly line. Lily and Eileen stayed inside reading or mending clothes in the evenings. And Pa, well Pa, wasn't quite the same since his indictment. He'd taken to sitting for hours in his chair by the fire watching the flames flicker. He must have seen something there that brought solace is all I could figure. I'd try to encourage him to come out and join us but he'd mumble a "No thanks," or something to the effect of his needing to think.

One evening as we were working on building the fourth pair, Sophie spoke up, "What's going to happen if Pa gets sent to jail? Who's going to take care of us? I wish we'd never asked Mr. Burton to build the mirror or the ski lodge. Pa wouldn't be indicted for arson if we hadn't gone and meddled in things we shouldn't be meddling in."

"I know what you mean Sophie," Mica chimed in. "We wouldn't be in this mess if it weren't for Tommy and Tia's big idea to build that stupid mirror. Heck, we lived without it for all these years. I'm sure we could continue to get along without it. It'd be better to be in the dark with Pa than to be in the light without him.

I looked at Tommy to see if he was going to speak up, but he was speechless for a change. So I figured I'd better say something to squelch the uprising. "Look, you don't think Tommy and I haven't thought about all of those things you're spewing? You think we feel good about the way things have turned out?

Well, I can't speak for Tommy, but I haven't been sleeping well, and I can barely focus on my work for fear of what might happen to Pa and eventually to us if he doesn't win this case. But, may I remind you that you all agreed to doing this, so don't go blaming us.

I propose we keep praying for a good outcome and keep our ears open. Eventually, somebody is going to say something that will be the key to finding the real culprit. I feel it in my bones that this is going to come out in our favor. We've got to keep the faith."

"I hope to God you're right, Tia," Luca said as we continued sawing and scraping wood.

It wasn't long before my words proved true. Lorenzo rushed into my office one afternoon and said, "Tia, you won't believe what I heard today at work!"

"What? Is it about the case?"

"Yes, is anyone else around? Is it safe to talk?" Lorenzo asked.

"There is no one else here. It's been so quiet lately since Pa's been accused of arson."

"You better have a seat," Lorenzo said.

Lorenzo started, "I was waiting for instructions for the day with the other workers in the employee shed. The shed is a place near where we work on the mountain. It's used to store equipment and to warm up, so we meet there every morning. Usually, our lead will tell us what we're doing, but once in a while, Mr. Burton comes to rally the troops, so to speak," Lorenzo rolled his eyes.

"We were told to go all the way over to the west side of the mountain to put up safety fences to block the mounting snow from blowing onto the ski runs because it helps make skiing safer. Nobody was happy about the assignment because it was so cold. I was standing next to the Ricci brothers, Juan and Angelo. Do you know them?"

"No, I don't think I do. Are they workers from Milan?" I asked.

"Yes, they live in the dorms with the others. I get the impression they knew Burton from Milan. We've become working buddies; I really like them. Anyway, this morning, Angelo calls Burton a liar under his breath while Burton is giving his speech. I asked Angelo what he meant, and he said he'd tell me later. While checking each other for frostbite, I asked Angelo what he meant about Burton being a liar."

"Wait, what? You check each other for frostbite? What does that mean?" I asked.

"When it's freezing, and today was subzero with the wind chill factor, we all have to take fifteen minutes out of every hour to warm and check for frostbite in our hands and feet. Our supervisor makes us check each other because being objective about ourselves is difficult. Some people overreact and think they have frostbite, and some don't want the attention, so they don't report it. He says it's better if we have buddies check each other. Angelo, Juan, and I are 'frostbite-checking buddies,' which gives us time to talk about other stuff."

"Wow, what a good idea. I never would have thought to do that. Do you want some tea?" I asked, reaching for the tea kettle warming on the wood stove.

"Ok, sure. As I was saying, Angelo whispered that he and Juan were taking a shortcut through the woods one morning a while ago because they were running late. They heard voices and saw Mr. Burton and Jaden arguing, so they stopped and hid in the bushes. They didn't want Mr. Burton to see them arriving late to work, plus they could tell it was a heated discussion, and it would be embarrassing for everyone if they walked in on their conversation. They were close enough to overhear what Mr. Burton and Jaden were saying.

As I leaned in to make sure I caught every word, I saw Lorenzo's eyebrows raise. "Tia!" he exclaimed as I followed his eyes to my lap, where I was bobbing the tea bag on my knee, missing the cup of hot water. We both chuckled as he continued.

"Angelo said Mr. Burton told Jaden he had to keep quiet about the avalanche accident because it would be all over if anybody found out. With how compliant Jaden usually is with his dad, Juan said he couldn't believe Jaden was actually talking back to his father. He said Jaden was livid. Jaden accused his dad of trying to kill him. Burton then went on to say how he had the ambulances there just in case and how he knew it wouldn't be a bad avalanche because there wasn't that much snow, that is, before the snowstorm the night before.

But by then, everything was set in place, and delay was not an option. He tried convincing Jaden that he had done it all for him because the whole town would belong to Jaden one day. He said once your Pa was out of the way, Mr. Burton would easily take over. Plus, Mr. Burton said no one would ever believe that he was the one who set the fire, knowing his own son was out skiing at the time and might get caught in the avalanche."

"You mean to tell me that Mr. Burton was the one who set the fire and caused the explosion? I asked in shock. "And he knew Jaden was skiing at the time!"

"That's exactly what I am saying," Lorenzo answered.

"Oh my gosh! Poor Jaden," I said. "Why would Mr. Burton even tell Jaden that he did it?"

"I don't know; maybe Jaden suspected his dad had something to do with it and confronted him. Angelo and Juan didn't hear that part of the conversation," Lorenzo added.

"I told them not to tell a soul what they just told me. I said if Mr. Burton catches even a whiff that they overheard his conversation with Jaden, they could both be in big trouble. If he's willing to compromise his own son to further his agenda, think about what he might do to them."

"No kidding!" I said in disbelief.

Lorenzo continued, "I told them I was going to talk to you about it. They wondered why I wouldn't tell my dad since he's the sheriff. I said we need to think this through before we go telling the authorities because of the danger this could put them in. They were so relieved to hear me say that because they had been struggling with knowing who to trust."

"This is just the break we need," I said. "But poor Jaden. Can you imagine having your own father betray you like that?"

"Yeah, I guess that is pretty bad, but I'm worried about the Ricci brothers. How do we keep Burton from finding out," Lorenzo said. "What do you think we should do?"

"I'm thinking. Give me a minute," I said, rubbing my chin.

"How about we take a trip to Milan and talk with Jaden? If I can talk him into it, maybe he'd be willing to testify in court. That way, Angelo and Juan never have to say a word," I said. "Jaden would be a credible witness."

"Why don't we just try to talk to him here? Isn't he staying at the old Luther place with his dad?" Lorenzo asked.

"I don't know; I think Jaden is in Milan. I haven't seen him since the accident. Pa went by there the other day to see how Jaden was doing, and Mr. Burton yelled at him to get away from his property—he said that Jaden went back to Milan. I'm sure we can ask around at the Hotel Rosi about Jaden's whereabouts. Can you get away this Saturday? Can we take your truck?" I asked.

"Sure, I'll tell my dad we're going to pick up a few things from town. He'll never suspect a thing. But no other brothers and sisters can come for obvious reasons," Lorenzo responded.

That Saturday was a glorious morning as we headed off for Milan. "I think this is the first time we've ever traveled this distance by ourselves," I said.

"I think you're right." Lorenzo squeezed my hand as I sat beside him.

Despite the paved road, we jiggled and bumped along in Mr. Leoni's truck. The gasoline smell was pungent at first until I got used to it. I loved snuggling close to Lorenzo under the blanket we brought since the heater was needed to defrost the windshield. The heat emanating from our bodies kept us warm and melted the crystals on the side windows. I watched, mesmerized, as the water dripped, distracting my thoughts.

"Are you nervous about being a detective?" Lorenzo asked.

"We're not detectives, are we?"

"What else would you call what we are doing?" Lorenzo wondered.

"Well, we are merely trying to find an old friend to see if he is all right," I reasoned.

"Oh, that's a nice way of putting it."

"Well, it's true," I said. "Plus, if I look at it like that, I don't get so nervous."

"If we do find Jaden and I get a chance to talk to him, what should I say? How should I say it? Should I tell him we know what really happened? If I do, then I'll have to trust he won't tell his dad," Tia rambled.

"I think you'll find the words you need to say, Tia; you always do," Lorenzo said reassuringly.

"Well, here we are at Burton's hotel. Good luck," Lorenzo said.

"Oh, thanks; you're just going to let me go in alone?"

"You'll be fine. Just say you're a friend in town from Dark Valley and wanted to say hi to Jaden," Lorenzo suggested.

"Good idea! I knew I brought you along for more reasons than your good looks and your truck," I chided.

"Stick with me, baby, and I'll show you things you've only imagined," Lorenzo laughed.

Walking through the glass rotating door brought back memories of my first visit. I was surprised by how things seemed smaller and lackluster. I wondered if the dinginess was real or a result of my knowledge of all the corruption behind the wealth. Even the previously impressive glass chandeliers now hung like gaudy reflections of the insincerity of everything pertaining to Mr. Burton.

"Wow, that was fast," Lorenzo said. "I didn't even have time to get bored."

"Drive around to the back alley. Stop like you're making a delivery to one of the businesses up from the hotel. We might be able to follow them to where Jaden is. The guy behind the bar told me he didn't know where Jaden was. I could tell he was lying. He thought I had left, but I hid around the doorpost and listened in. Luckily, the place was empty. I heard him ask the cook when the food would be ready for Jaden. They will be delivering his meal soon. All we have to do is not get noticed and follow them to where Jaden is," I said.

"Oh my gosh, this is crazy," Lorenzo said. "Do you think we should be doing this?"

"What's the worst that could happen? Stay far enough behind them so they don't see us," I advised.

"I've never followed someone before. This is nerve-wracking," Lorenzo said.

"There they go in that delivery van." I motioned to Lorenzo to start driving. We drove down this barely visible dirt road covered by low-hanging trees. It was dark and spooky.

"They're slowing down, pulling into that driveway. Stop here. Pull in behind these bushes," I said.

"OK, Tia, you don't have to tell me every little step. I think I'm smart enough to know to hide the truck," Lorenzo said.

"Sorry, I'm nervous. What if something happens inside where you can't see me? What if he has a gun and shoots me?" I said.

"First of all, it's Jaden we're talking about. He's not going to shoot you. If any of his father's goons are around, don't go in; just say you're sorry. You have the wrong address. He's probably alone, so you'll just have to feel him out to know what and how much to say. You know what I mean? I'm right here if anything should happen," Lorenzo tried to reassure me.

But I wasn't reassured. We had come all this way; there was no turning back now. I buttoned my coat to my chin, hoping the tightness around my throat would fortify me. Inching myself from the front seat to the frigid air, my breath came out in a cloud as I sighed. My usual confident self must have taken a vacation because try as I might, I couldn't find her. So, I located my next best self—the one who makes light of stressful situations. I imagined Jaden in his pj's sipping hot chocolate alone and excitedly welcoming me in. I told myself I was being absolutely ridiculous. Jaden cares about me; even Miss May said so.

The delivery guy was long gone as I timidly walked down the path to the house that sat a great distance off the road, hidden behind a small forest. "*Some cabin,*" I thought. I felt tiny next to the massive wooden door with a large wooden knocker. The knocker was so high up I could just barely lift it with my longest finger, and I let it go with a thud. I did it several more times. I supposed the reverberation through the woods echoed through the house as well. I regretted knocking so much, fearing I'd awaken or alert something I shouldn't. I was just about to leave when the door barely opened. The sunlight fit perfectly through the break in the trees, nearly blinding Jaden. Shielding his eyes with his hand, Jaden refocused to see me standing there.

Jaden said, "Tia, what are you doing here?" He looked like he hadn't bathed or changed his clothes since the accident. It was almost 1:00 p.m., and yet it appeared he had just awakened.

Softly, I said, "Jaden, it's good to see you. Are you ok?"

Jaden replied, "You came all the way from Dark Valley to ask me how I am doing?" The door started to close slowly, giving me just enough time to put my foot in the doorway.

I quickly said, "Can we talk?"

"Talk about what? What's there to talk about?" Jaden said.

"I didn't know what happened to you after the avalanche. I ran down to the town hall looking for you, but you weren't there. Then you just disappeared. I was worried about you."

"Well, you can see I'm just fine, so kindly remove your foot," Jaden said.

"Please, Jaden, just a few minutes. I really need to talk to you," I said in my most urgent voice.

"Oh, alright, but just a few minutes. You'll have to excuse the mess; I wasn't expecting company," Jaden said sarcastically, moving some papers off a chair for me and opening one curtain panel to let in some light.

The small streak of sunlight illuminated the room just enough that I could see that it looked more like a wrestling ring than a living room. All the furniture, except for one beautifully embroidered couch, was upside down or strewn with debris. The one upright couch was covered with pillows and a comforter. I assumed it served as Jaden's bed. The smell was dank and foul as if an illness clung to the walls. Instead of holding my nose shut, I pulled my sweater up over it for a moment until I adjusted to the stench.

"I'm so glad to see you and that you're ok. Well, are you ok? Did you recover from the accident?" I asked.

Jaden said, "I'm still recovering, but I am better than I was."

"Good to hear. When will you be returning to the valley? Do you know?"

Jaden said emphatically, "Never. I won't ever be going back there. I'm done with the valley."

"Not even when the ski lodge is complete?" I asked.

"No, not even then."

I spoke softly yet firmly, "Jaden, look, a couple of guys from the ski mountain overheard you and your dad talking in the woods about what really happened the day of the avalanche. We know the truth. I am so sorry that your dad put you in that position. I can't imagine how you must be feeling. And now, it all makes sense why you left. And, well, everything makes sense."

Jaden replied frantically, "Oh my gosh, I can't believe what you're telling me. You know?"

I nodded yes, allowing him some space to process what he had just heard.

Jaden continued, "So that's why you're here? I should have known you didn't come to see how I was. You came to see what? If I will testify?! You've got a lot of nerve. You can leave now."

I quickly responded, "Jaden, just hear me out. This could be one of the biggest decisions you'll ever make. Do you really want to spend the rest of your life living in your father's shadow? Do you really want to live with this on your conscience? Can you live with yourself, knowing that your testimony could exonerate an innocent man? You'd rather continue living with your father ordering you around? Look, this is exactly the time to stand up to your father. Look what he did to you. He put you in the path of danger to promote himself. I know that's difficult to come to terms with. But you don't have to live under his control anymore."

"Well, you got those two guys who overheard the conversation. They're going to testify, right? So why do you need me?" Jaden quickly responded.

I hoped my heartfelt response would be hard to resist. "The jury might not believe Lorenzo's friends. It would be a couple of minimum wage employees' words against Mr. Burton, the owner of Northwest Engineering Company. We need your testimony to make it believable. Please, Jaden, you really are our only hope."

Jaden replied, "You don't know what you're asking me. My father owns most of Milan and Sicily. He could make my life a living hell if I ever told the truth. Do you think he's just going to lie down? He'll twist the truth like he always does and get his way. "

I encouraged Jaden by saying, "Maybe you could be put in a witness protection plan. Eventually, you're going to want your independence. Look at you. You're holed up in your house, afraid to come out."

Jaden yelled, "You don't know anything! You know very little about my life, and I'd like to see what you would do in my position! I don't have people who will shelter me like you do; I have no one! It's just me and my father!"

"Jaden, many people have tried to be your friend, but you scare them away. Lots of people would want to help you," I continued.

"Like who?"

"Well, Lorenzo, for one, and Luca and Mica. Heck, my whole family would."

Jaden stopped for a minute to think of a rebuttal but said, "Really, people like me and want to be my friend? Hmm. Well, I'm not buying it, and there is no way I will testify against my father for obvious reasons and because I don't want everyone in the world to know what a loser I am. It's humiliating to even think about it. Now I would like you to leave. Look, you have to promise you won't tell a soul you saw me. No one can know where I am, especially not your father's lawyer. Promise me, Tia," Jaden said, going for the door.

I stood up and said, "I promise. You have my word. Every one of us has been betrayed by someone. Some of us have even been betrayed by our own fathers. You're not alone in that. You could have a home in the valley with lots of friends or live a lonely life under your father's control. It's your choice." With that, I slowly walked through the threshold, hoping Jaden might change his mind. But instead, he slammed the door.

Walking quickly back to the truck, I jumped in and told Lorenzo to drive fast. Lorenzo already had the truck facing in the same direction as we had come so we could find our way back. I felt like I held my breath for a long time, thinking somehow that not breathing would keep us hidden. Maybe it did because no one seemed to notice us as we headed back home on the paved two-lane highway while I recounted the whole interaction with Jaden to Lorenzo.

"Wow, Tia, you did a great job laying it out there. If that doesn't make him testify, then I don't know what would."

I sadly replied, "Yeah, but I may have pushed too hard. Maybe I made it worse."

"No, I think you said the right thing. He needed to hear it," Lorenzo said.

The drive home seemed longer than the drive down. There wasn't much else to say.

CHAPTER 15
And the Verdict is?

Lorenzo and I thought we should stop by Jaden's house two days before the trial to see if he'd changed his mind. Seeing a strange car in the driveway and hearing raised voices, we decided to peek through the window where the curtain was open. We saw and heard Jaden having a heated conversation with two men in cheap suits. The short and stocky one seemed to have a personality like his hair, which was plastered to his head except for one strand that stood straight up. The lanky one seemed a little nearsighted, much like his pants that were too short.

The smaller man said, "Hey, Jaden, how's things going? We haven't seen you around lately, and your father asked us to check in and see how you're doing. We even brought you some lasagna from the restaurant. You doing ok? How have you been? I think your dad is real worried about you."

"Yeah, Vinney, I'm ok. Just recuperating from the accident. Thanks for the lasagna. This will be great. I'm getting kind of sick of eating pork and beans." Jaden combed his fingers through his hair and tried to smooth out the wrinkles in his shirt by rubbing his hands over the creases like an iron would do. But it didn't have the same effect.

Then the taller guy chimed in, "Yeah, we heard a dame came by the restaurant looking for you a while back. What was that all about? Did you talk to her? Who was she? Some bunny you met in the mountains? Hey, you can tell us." The guy slapped Jaden on his arm like they were buddies.

Jaden pulled away and replied, "None of your business, Fredo."

They both closed in on Jaden, getting right in his face. Jaden's slight flinch made me think Vinney's breath was as bad as his hairstyle. Otherwise, Jaden stood perfectly still, staring through him.

Vinney said, "If we catch wind of you hanging around that dame from the valley, we have been ordered to take you far, far away. What's her name, Tia? You are forbidden to see her or anyone from that town. You got it?"

Jaden didn't budge. Fredo took Jaden's shirt collar, pulled it tight, and said, "You got that, pretty boy? We don't want to catch you going anywhere near that place."

Jaden reluctantly said, "I got it; now let me go."

Fredo loosened his grip, saying, "Glad we have an understanding."

As they were leaving, Vinney said, "Oh, by the way, your Pa said as soon as the trial is over, you and he can take a nice long trip on his boat. Just the two of you—go fishing and all. So he can make it up to you. A nice father-son vacation. That sounds real nice, don't it? You're a lucky boy to have such a good dad. You know that, right?"

Lorenzo and I ducked low behind the bushes and waited for the two thugs to drive away. Then we let ourselves in.

"Jaden, are you all right? I'm sorry, but we saw the whole thing," I said.

"Am I glad to see you! I've had it with my father and these hooligans threatening me like I'm some sort of criminal. Like they own me. I'm ready to testify," Jaden declared, surprising himself.

"Oh my gosh, Jaden, that's fantastic!" Lorenzo said.

"This is the best news ever," I said, giving Jaden the biggest hug, which seemed to seal the deal. My heart melted just a little, and I thought, given different circumstances, I could have easily fallen for Jaden. But there was too much between Lorenzo and me for that ever to happen.

"Lorenzo, can you drive your truck around back to give me time to pack a few things?" Jaden asked. "Tia, can you help me pack? I feel an extra pair of eyes would be useful. I may never be able to come back here again, and I want to make sure I have everything I need."

"I wouldn't be so sure about that, Jaden. Your father may be in jail for a while, which may leave you with many options," I said with a huge grin.

We drove quietly, hoping we would not be detected through the back roads. Once we were far enough north of the town and back on the main road, we all seemed to relax a little. What an amazing turn of events, driving back with Jaden, who was the answer to our prayers. And I hoped we could be the answers to his prayers.

My daydreaming of how I loved Lorenzo and my strong friendship with Jaden was interrupted when Jaden asked, "Don't you think we should have a plan about my returning to the valley and speaking at the trial? I don't really want my dad to know I'm here or what I'm about to do."

"There's a closet in our barn where you can sleep. If we fill it with hay all around the floors and up the walls, it stays pretty warm in there. I know; I've done it many times," Lorenzo offered.

"I don't know. Jaden's not really acclimated to our weather like us. Plus, he'll need to eat, and we can't hide him all day in the barn," I said.

"What if you invite Miss May to stay in your house for a few days because of some repairs that need to be done? You can make something up. Then Jaden will have a safe, private, warm place to stay until the trial," Lorenzo said.

"Perfect, except for where am I going to put Miss May in my house? There is no room.

Never mind, I'll think of something. Maybe I'll give her my bed, and I'll sleep on the couch in the living room. I know I won't be sleeping very well anyway with the trial coming up," I mused.

"Ok, now that's settled, how are we going to handle the trial itself? Should we tell your dad's lawyer that I want to testify?" Jaden asked.

"I'm pretty sure he's obliged to tell the judge and Mr. Burton's lawyer about your testimony. We can't chance it," I said.

"Well, what if I just appear at the last minute after everyone else has testified but before closing arguments? I can just pretend that I showed up out of the blue to testify and that you two didn't know anything about it. That may be the only way this will work," Jaden said.

"That's not a bad idea. What do you think, Tia?" Lorenzo asked.

"We'll have to pray for a miracle. From what I've learned listening to Mr. Chambers, my dad's lawyer, judges don't like surprises. But maybe you'd be a big enough surprise to make it worth the court's time.

Sitting around the dinner table the night before the trial was like eating with an inmate at his last meal. It was a solemn occasion except for Miss May's continual chatter, a pleasant diversion from our jittery nerves. I made a mental note to myself to tell Miss May that she is more than welcome to come to dinner every night once she is back in her own home. I can't believe none of us thought of it before.

Pa was quieter than usual while maintaining a stiff upper lip. But I could tell he was hurting. He was probably more worried about us than himself because that's just how he was. I ate supper fast and excused myself to feed Jeb. I put the leftovers in a pot, which was actually for Jaden, and headed over to Miss May's.

"How's it going?" I asked.

"I'm going a little stir-crazy, but it's given me time to think about what I will say tomorrow on the stand. I've been writing down some details to help me remember what to say that I hadn't thought of before. Does anyone suspect I'm here?" Jaden asked.

"No, no one suspects a thing. They're all too busy thinking about their own part in the trial. None of us believed in even the slightest possibility of a guilty verdict. That is too much even to consider. Have you given any thought as to how you're going to make your big entrance tomorrow?" I asked.

"Every other thought is about how I will approach Mr. Chambers. Maybe he'll need to get something from his car during the trial, or he'll need to take a break, and I'll be waiting for him there. What do you think? Tell me what his car looks like," Jaden said.

The house was quiet when I returned. Despite my tiptoeing up the stairs to get my nightgown, Miss May was awake, waiting for me. "Did Jaden enjoy the leftovers you brought him?" Miss May asked.

"What do you mean?" I asked stupidly.

"I know he's hiding in my house so he can testify tomorrow," Miss May smiled.

"Shhh, don't tell anyone, Miss May; please, promise me you won't," I whispered as I sat next to her on the bed. "How did you know?"

"I may be shortsighted, but I'm pretty good at putting two and two together. I figured it doesn't take two hours to feed Jeb. I won't say a word to anyone," Miss May said.

"I hope you don't mind being moved out of your house for a few days. We couldn't think of any other safe place to put Jaden."

"No, dear, I don't mind, but next time, just ask me. I'm a good secret keeper. I'm happy to help your Pa in whatever way I can, and I'm glad to be playing a part, however small."

"Well, we didn't want to put you in any danger either. The less everybody knows, the better," I said.

"You're a good daughter, Tia. Smart, too. Nobody else would do what you've done. Actually, no one else has even thought of doing what you did. I'm coming tomorrow. I wouldn't miss it for the world."

Miss May gave me a big hug. I buried my head in her shoulder, feeling like crying buckets right then, but I didn't want to wake anyone, so I found my strong self—the one who wiped the lone tear sliding down my face.

"Thank you, Miss May, for noticing. You amaze me. I only hope I will be half as on top of things at your age as you are," I said as I gave her one more squeeze before heading to my bed on the couch.

The court was packed when we arrived. Lorenzo, Angelo, and Juan saved us room in the front row, sitting right behind Pa. Reaching across the railing which separated the defendant from the audience, I put my hand on Pa's shoulder. He turned around, placing his hand top of mine. I was surprised to see him smiling. I couldn't believe how calm he seemed.

"It's going to be ok, Tia. They don't have any evidence. This is all a show for Burton to be a big dog, but I think it will backfire in his face," Pa said.

"I believe you are right, Pa. I believe you are right," I said, letting go of his shoulder and sitting back against the hard wooden bench.

"All rise," the bailiff announced as the judge walked in.

Scanning the room as everyone rose, I could see there wasn't an empty seat in the room. I noticed the Duces, Gus, Ed, and Mr. Waller, and I saw a familiar face from the corner of my eye. Why, it was Miss Fiora. She saw me look her way and stared at me hard like she wanted to say something. She eventually nodded in resignation as everyone sat before the trial started. She knew there was no time to speak with me right then.

The prosecuting attorney, Mr. Pagano, first called Mr. Burton to take the stand. It was as difficult to sit there and listen to his testimony as it is to sit still on Fridays in May at school. I brought my notebook so I could draw people testifying and take notes or just doodle. I drew Mr. Burton with beady eyes and smoke curling from his nostrils and ears. I twitched with every lie. Eileen elbowed me every time I jerked. I couldn't move over anymore without crushing Sophie. I didn't purposefully jerk; it was just my body's way of sloughing off the fallacies, which tried to stick like a sweaty shirt on a hot summer's day. The judge also found a place in my notebook. He was an interesting man from Milan with a white mustache and white curly hair who reminded me of Mark Twain. His accent led me to believe he wasn't Italian at all, perhaps originally from France. He seemed irritated when things went slowly. I imagined he was the type who would rather be fishing than hearing this ridiculous case. I had no way of knowing that for sure, but I thought, if it were true, it could work in our favor.

The day proceeded with a lunch break and then testimony from all the accident victims. This gave me a wealth of items to sketch. Each victim was unique, with varying degrees of injuries due to the avalanche. A few were from Milan, but most lived in Dark Valley. It was interesting to listen to each of them, but I wondered how this had anything to do with who had done it. They knew nothing about who started the fire. Each of them heard the explosion and were caught in the avalanche. But a thought popped into my head, which was a eureka moment. If Mr. Pagano questioned each and every victim, he was missing one...Jaden. This is perfect! They will have a perfect reason to question him. He was probably already on the witness list. I got butterflies in my stomach again, and now I could really not sit still, hoping it would soon be over.

I ran past Sophie as soon as court closed for the day, hoping to catch Jaden to tell him. He was sitting in Mr. Chambers' car just like he said he would do. I signaled to him with a wave of my hand to come and follow me so we wouldn't be seen. We ran from there all the way back to Miss May's place.

"Is it over already for the day?" Jaden asked, sounding a bit confused.

"Jaden, it's perfect! I think this is going to really work. And yes, it's over for the day. You didn't miss much. Your father testified, and then every victim from the avalanche. A couple of them were still in casts with bruises still showing. But the best part is, if Mr. Pagano had all of them on the witness list, your name would likely be on it, too. Which means Mr. Chambers has every reason to call you to the stand without any explanation!" I practically shouted. I was so excited.

"Oh wow, I guess you're right," Jaden said, looking perplexed.

"I think we need to get Mr. Chambers over here to talk with you tonight before trial tomorrow. He'll know what to do. They'll probably present the glove tomorrow, which won't amount to a hill of beans. Then, Mr. Chambers will be calling witnesses. What do you say? Do you want to talk to Mr. Chambers? Oh, and by the way, Miss May knows you're staying in her house. But she promised not to tell anyone, and I believe her," I said.

"Yes, I think that makes sense. Can we run this by Lorenzo first to get his take on it? I need a little time to process all of this," Jaden said.

"Ok, sure. I'll go see if he's back yet," I said.

After all the back and forth about whether we should tell Mr. Chambers or not, we decided to go ahead and tell him since he would probably be coming over to discuss the trial anyway. We were relieved when we saw his car pull into the driveway.

He always seemed to come right when dinner was served, so we put another plate on the table. Luca ate fast and went out to do something, probably just to breathe and calm his nerves. After tidying things up, I asked Mr. Chambers and Pa to come to Miss May's because I had something to show them. I wished I had a camera to record the look on Mr. Chambers' face when he saw Jaden. Pa was shocked and shaken when told the truth of what happened.

"This is the best news ever!" Mr. Chambers exclaimed. "I'll put you on the stand tomorrow, Jaden, and this whole nonsense will be over. We'll keep you hidden until you're to take the stand. Maybe you can hide in my car, but you must lie on the floor. I'll send Tia out to get you when it's time. The element of surprise will benefit Rubin greatly. You're a strong young man to testify against your father. Your father will be in jail for quite a while, so you shouldn't have to worry about any ramifications."

The next morning, Mr. Chambers picked up Jaden, hiding him with a blanket in the back of his car. Walking into the courthouse, I saw Miss Fiora waiting by the front steps.

"Hello, Miss Fiora, so good to see you. How have you been?" I said.

"Tia, you've grown into a beautiful young lady. I feel terrible about how things have turned out for your family. I wonder if you realize that Mr. Burton is probably behind this whole mess? I don't have any evidence; I just know how he operates. Is there anything I can do to help?" Miss Fiora asked.

"No worries, Clarissa; we've got it all figured out, I think. I'm so glad you are here to witness a marvelous outcome of this whole mess," I said, smiling.

Clarissa's face changed to a quizzical smile. "Maybe we could talk after the trial," Miss Clarissa said.

"Why don't you come over to our house afterward? I think we'll be celebrating," I said.

"Well, sure," Clarissa responded with the same quizzical look.

Everyone was shocked when Mr. Chambers called Jaden to the stand. Mr. Burton's startled expression was particularly satisfying: three parts disbelief, three parts anger, three parts panic, I surmised.

There was some discussion between the lawyers and the judge about how Jaden wasn't on the witness list, so why was he here to testify? The prosecuting attorney had not had an opportunity to vet him thoroughly.

Mr. Chambers rebutted the argument by saying, "Jaden was on the initial witness list. It's not our fault if you didn't vet him. I'm sure you would have had access to him since he is Mr. Burton's son."

The judge thought for a few minutes and said, "I will allow him to testify today."

The bailiff said, "State your full name for the record."

"Jaden Allister Burton"

Bailiff spoke clearly and to the point, "Put your right hand on the Bible and repeat after me."

"I solemnly swear to tell the whole truth and nothing but the truth, so help me God."

"You may be seated."

Sitting in the witness chair, Jaden looked small. I smiled at him, hoping to encourage him. He smiled back carefully.

Mr. Chambers asked, "Jaden, how are you related to Mr. Burton?

Jaden said, "He's my father."

Mr. Chambers said, "In your own words, could you please tell the court what happened the day of the avalanche."

Jaden explained how he had been skiing all morning. "It was about 11:30 a.m. when I heard an explosion, like the ones you hear early in the morning or late in the evening. But you never hear them in the middle of the day. I was wondering what was going on."

"What are these explosions, as you called them, supposed to do?"

Jaden explained, "They are meant to start an avalanche to make the ski hill safe for skiing. If too much snow has built up and the skiers come onto the mountain, the vibrations from the skiers could initiate an avalanche.

"Can you explain how dangerous avalanches are?" Mr. Chambers asked.

"They can kill you. The force of an avalanche can knock you over, leaving you covered in snow, like a grave," Jaden continued.

"What was it like for you? What happened after you heard the explosion?

"I then heard rumbling and could feel the vibration. I quickly looked up the mountain and saw the wave of snow heading my way. I skied as quickly as I could, but the snow was faster, and it overtook me near the bottom of the hill. I was one of the lucky ones who was found first. I wasn't completely buried, so it was easy for them to find me. I only incurred a sprained ankle."

"I'm sorry you were caught in the avalanche, and we are so glad to see you've recovered. Do you happen to know who set the fire that day?" Mr. Chambers asked in a gentle yet firm voice.

"Yes, I do."

"And how do you know?"

"Because the person who did it told me so."

"Is that person in the courtroom today?"

"Yes, he is."

"Could you please point to him and say his name for the record?"

Jaden pointed directly at his father and said, "My father, Mr. John Burton."

The sound of the gavel pierced the gasps and shouts of people, along with the judge shouting, "Order in the court! There will be order in the court!" The courtroom quieted. "You may continue, Mr. Chambers."

"Please continue, Jaden."

"I thought Mr. Scalini did it like everyone was saying. I really didn't think about it anymore. Until one day, my dad and I were talking on the way to the ski hill. My dad was going to talk with the workers who were putting up fences to help corral the snow.

As we were talking, my dad slipped. He thought he was being funny and said, 'We don't want another avalanche to happen, so we better have the guys put up some fences.' I asked him, 'So fences help to keep the snow from avalanching?' I was confused. *'Why hadn't this been done before?'* I wondered. He said, 'Oh yeah, putting up snow barriers in strategic places can help to keep an avalanche from happening.' I asked my dad why we hadn't done this before, and he said, 'Well, we weren't ready.' I said, 'Ready? Ready for what?' 'For me to take over the town. But now we are, so we can work on the ski hill to make it safer.'

I kept pressing my dad about what he meant about taking over the town. And then he told me the whole tale of how he detonated the dynamite near the time of the furnace exploding to mask the sound. He assumed the avalanche wouldn't be too big but just enough to cause some drama. He said he didn't expect anyone to be hurt at all but misjudged the amount of snow."

"And what about you, Jaden? Did your father know you were skiing at the time?"

"Yes, he said he knew I was skiing and where I was on the hill, and he thought I would be able to get down before any damage happened. He thought my involvement would keep him above suspicion. Although he said he didn't think I would get hurt. He said he did it for me so that I could take over the town when I got older."

"Jaden, thank you for being so candid about what you know. This couldn't have been easy for you to come forward. I have no further questions, your honor."

Mr. Pagano stood up slowly and walked toward Jaden. There wasn't a sound in the courtroom. It was as if everyone held their breath, not wanting to miss a thing.

"Well, well, Jaden. Aren't you the big savior? Coming forward at the last minute to testify against your father. After all your father has done for you, this is how you repay him? You should be ashamed of yourself."

Before Mr. Pagano could finish the sentence, Mr. Chambers shouted, "I object, your honor. This is irrelevant."

"Sustained. Those remarks will be stricken from the record. Mr. Pagano, let's keep it clean. No more chastising."

"Yes, your honor. Jaden, this is just your word against your father's word. I could easily put your father on the stand again to refute your words. It is highly suspect that a man of Mr. Burton's caliber could devise such a sinister scheme. Do you really expect the jury to believe what you are saying?"

"Don't take my word for it; ask Angelo and Juan Ricci. They overheard the whole conversation. They were late getting to work the day my dad and I were having the conversation in the woods, and they overheard the whole conversation and are willing to testify if called upon."

"Are you telling the court that if we interview Angelo and Juan Ricci, they will corroborate your testimony?

"That's exactly what I am saying."

"In light of this new evidence, your honor, I would ask for time to interrogate, I mean, interview the witnesses," Mr. Pagano said.

The judge responded, "In light of this new evidence, I am dropping the charges against Mr. Scalini and arresting Mr. Burton. He will be held in the town jail until we can sort this whole thing out."

"I object, your honor!" Mr. Pagano screeched.

"I'm sure you do, Mr. Pagano. My ruling stands. I want to see both attorneys in my office, pronto. Court dismissed."

The officer on duty handcuffed Mr. Burton and took him through the doors to the jail adjacent to the courtroom. With that, Mr. Chambers and Mr. Pagano went through the entrance to the judge's chambers to discuss the newly developed situation.

"So, tell me, Mr. Chambers, what just happened in my courtroom? Did you intentionally try to mislead me and Mr. Pagano?" the judge asked.

"No, your honor. It's like I told you. Jaden was originally on the witness list, but when I couldn't find him, I figured we had enough witnesses testifying about the accident. I didn't see a need to pursue him, especially since he is Mr. Burton's son. I figured there was no way I would ever get any information worth pursuing. Mr. Pagano never said anything about me striking him from the witness list. He just happened to show up today out of the blue. Everyone seemed surprised to see him."

"Mr. Pagano, were you aware of any of this?"

"No, your honor."

"OK, what's to say we reconvene in two days? That should give you enough time to interview the new witnesses," the judge said.

"Excuse me, your honor, with all due respect. Could we make it one day?"

"Why, Mr. Chambers? You better have a good reason to ask me that."

"Your Honor, I do. I fear for the safety of Angelo and Juan Ricci.

"From whom?"

"Mr. Burton. If it's true, and I believe it is, that Mr. Burton intentionally put his son in danger to frame Rubin Scalini, what's to keep him from harming Angelo and Juan? Their testimonies could seal the case. Don't you think Mr. Burton will be posting bail shortly?"

"I set bail at 100,000 lira, Mr. Chambers. I don't think Mr. Burton will be going anywhere. I have already thought of that possibility. Mr. Pagano, I'm sure one day will be enough time to interview the Ricci brothers. We will adjourn until the day after tomorrow."

"Thank you, your honor," Mr. Chambers said.

The last day of the trial was anti-climactic. Most believed the story Jaden told. When Angelo and Juan's testimony exactly matched Jaden's rendition, the trial was over. The jury came back quickly with a guilty verdict. Mr. Burton would be put away for quite some time for arson and malicious intent.

CHAPTER 16
La Fine

There was quite a celebration at our house the night Burton was taken to jail. We all assumed he would be incarcerated for a long time. The party spilled out into the yard from the jam-packed kitchen. Most congratulated Pa, and some even apologized for believing the worst about him. Pa clinked his glass with a spoon to get everyone's attention.

"I'd like to raise a toast to all the people who made my freedom possible. Thank you, Mr. Chambers, for representing me. Thank you to Angelo and Juan for telling the truth. Thank you to my family for all of your support. Here's to Tia and Lorenzo for their detective efforts to bring about a good ending. I wouldn't be standing here right now if it weren't for your tenacity, ingenuity, and street smarts. I'd say you make a good private eye team."

Everyone raised their glasses and said, "*Come dire applausi quando si beve,*" as they tapped their glasses together in agreement and celebration.

"There is one more person I'd like to thank—Jaden. Jaden, thank you for standing up and telling the truth, especially when you had so much to lose. You displayed great courage. We hope you and your father will be reconciled one day. But I want you to know, and I believe I speak for everyone, that you always have a place here. We hope you will consider Dark Valley as your home."

Again, everyone cheered and clapped. Many people patted Jaden on the back or gave him hugs. It was good to see Jaden getting congratulated and welcomed. I imagined he would need a new place to belong, especially now.

"Tia," Miss Fiora tapped me on the shoulder. "Seems like you knew what the outcome was going to be. Nice work!"

"Miss Fiora, I'm so happy you are here to celebrate with us. I really appreciate your support and for traveling all the way up here to help."

"Well, I didn't do much. But I'm glad I could be here to support you through such a difficult time. Plus, I wanted to let you know I'll be moving to Genoa to live with my niece. She and her husband bought a new place big enough to include me. I'm happy to be moving on. I wonder what will happen to the hotel now that Mr. Burton will be in jail. Do you think Jaden will run it and take over all of the business dealings?"

"I have no idea what Jaden is going to do. He will have so much to deal with now that his dad is in jail. Who knows how things will develop? I wonder who will manage the construction work on the hotel and the ski hill? We are kind of in a pickle, now that I think of it. I hadn't thought beyond the trial. Many decisions need to be made. But we'll deal with it like we do everything: together. It's exciting that you're moving to Genoa. I hope things go well for you there."

"You're welcome to come and visit any time. There is plenty of room for company in the house. You won't believe how beautiful Genoa is by the sea. There are copious opportunities for someone with your talent."

"Talent? What talent do I have?" Tia asked.

"Tia, I've seen the way you take notes. You are an excellent stenographer."

"Oh, that. No big deal."

"It looks like you created your own shortcut version to writing. It's very clever. You might even be able to start your own school and teach others. There is a high demand for stenographers," Clarissa said.

"I had no idea. I'll keep that in mind. And thanks for the compliment. I would like to visit you in Genoa. We would have fun. Make sure I give you my mailing address before you leave so we can stay in touch," Tia responded.

"Great! I would love for you to meet my niece. I think you two would hit it off."

After the crowd dwindled, we went inside and flopped in the living room, exhausted. Jaden spoke up and said, "I guess I'll go back to my place at the old Luther House so that Miss May can sleep in her own bed tonight.

"You'll do nothing of the sort. You stay as long as you want. We are getting used to this arrangement. Right, Tia?" Miss May said.

"Absolutely, Jaden. We love having you around," I said. "Really, we mean it. You stay as long as you like."

Pa chimed in, "Why don't we clean out the storage room next to the kitchen for a permanent room for Miss May? Then, Jaden can continue staying in the cottage. How does that sound to you, Miss May?"

"I love the idea! It's getting too difficult for me to live on my own," Miss May replied.

Thanks, I appreciate the offer. I sure don't want to go back to that Luther house by myself. That would be really depressing," Jaden said. "I don't even know where to begin with my new life. It feels strange to have options. I wonder who will manage the lodge's completion and run the ski hill?"

"I think you'd be the best choice," Pa suggested.

"Really, you think I can do it?" Jaden said.

"You betcha!" Pa reassured. "We are here to help. Maybe you could hire Lorenzo as an assistant if he would want."

"That might be fun!" Lorenzo shouted from across the room.

"You can drive my truck, and I'll get another one," Jaden responded.

Lorenzo squeezed my pinky so hard I thought I'd scream. Then he did something so unexpected. He kissed me in front of everyone. "I think it's time to make our dating official," Lorenzo declared. We kissed again, and most everyone clapped.

"Ok, you two love birds. That's not a surprise; just remember you're not married," Pa smiled.

"Yet!" Lorenzo replied.

"*What a perfect end to a perfect day,*" I thought as I cuddled even closer to Lorenzo!

MEET THE AUTHOR
Pauline Henning

Pauline Henning makes her home in Colorado. A retired teacher, critiquing literature with her students for twenty-three years afforded her a unique perspective when writing her first novel. I realized critiquing is far easier than writing.

Though growing up in Washington, D.C., her desire as a young person to be a farmer compelled her to look for greener pastures as soon as she was old enough. Not believing she could farm, she chose instead to content herself with growing flowers, herbs, and vegetables in a grow house, no easy feet at an elevation of 9,800 feet. She now spends her time caring for her plants followed by harvesting their best parts just before they expire. Like her plants, she is presently tending and harvesting her writing-self before completely retiring.

Made in the USA
Middletown, DE
28 January 2024

48314227R00096